WICKED JUSTICE

LORI RYAN

T.E. EDWARDS

BRIGHTON PARKER ROSE, LLC

CHAPTER 1

THE STENCH SEEPED FROM THE CRACKS OF THE OLD BUILDING, not so strong yet that a passerby on the sidewalk might notice, but to a trained detective's nose standing right at the front door, it was there. The unmistakable foul stench of decomposition that marred the crisp spring air of the sunny day and brought the sour taste of bile along for the ride.

Behind Detective Ronan Cafferty and his partner, on the other side of the red police tape and the yellow police tape farther out from that, unabashed gawkers had begun to gather, abandoning their morning destinations for the chance of seeing something grotesque. The murmurs told Ronan the crowd was piecing together bits of information about what had happened in the run-down four-story brick building in front of them.

He caught snippets of "security guard" and "dead guy was homeless." That was of course followed with "must be an overdose," because people always thought they knew everything about someone as soon as they got their hands on that someone's assigned label.

Zach Reynolds turned fully to face Ronan, though they

both knew what he was doing. His words of, "Ready to go in?" were nothing more than an excuse to scan the gathering for anyone who looked overly interested. Anyone who might be revisiting their own handiwork to take in the show. Ronan was doing the same with the people he could see, noticing that one man had stopped, despite the fact he had two small children in tow.

Fucking lovely. He caught the eye of the heavier of the two officers at the tape and tipped his head toward the kids. Ronan knew Spitz would do what Ronan would do if he wasn't about to enter the crime scene. He'd tell the asshole to get his kids out of there before they saw something they didn't need to see. The medical examiner was already on scene processing the body so it could be removed for autopsy.

Sure, the body would be sealed in a black bag, but it could still fuck with a kid's head. The idiot would thank Spitz when he wasn't sitting up with his terrified offspring after a midnight nightmare sent them screaming to Daddy's bed.

Ronan answered his partner's question by way of passing a small tin of mentholated rub to his partner. He'd already applied the harsh salve beneath his own nostrils, feeling the stubble he should have shaved clean with a razor that morning.

He'd been halfway dressed that morning when they got the call and had planned to use the electric razor he kept in his car to finish his morning routine. That failed when the razor turned out to still be dead because *batteries* was written on the long-overdue shopping list tucked in his wallet. The delinquent shopping list was the same reason he hadn't had breakfast.

In a related problem, the charcoal pants he wore had

been worn twice already that week and the burgundy button-down shirt once. He wasn't normally the kind of guy who sniffed out the least offensive of his laundry when getting dressed, but the week was getting away from him.

The homicide investigation they were now heading up wasn't going to aid him in wrangling it back under control.

Bits of concrete scuffed under their booted feet as they entered the old apartment building. Ronan recognized the *tink* of a screw or nail skittering over the checker-tiled floor in the entryway and they moved through to find the main space of the building had been gutted on the right side, further confirming his assessment that a construction crew had been there recently.

While the left side of the building still held the face of several apartments with numbered doors and wall sconces from the 1950s or worse, the right had been torn out from top to bottom with only metal framework and capped-off wires showing where the large space had once been divided into smaller units.

And it was literally top to bottom. The floor above them had been removed, along with most of the one above that and higher still. Rather than tear out the building and start clean, they were keeping the bones and fleshing it out new.

Ronan refocused on the entry level and took in their crime scene. Their victim was once a fair-haired, well-dressed white businessman in his late forties to early fifties. His body was now mangled and twisted, decorating the floor, a prominent welcome to anyone entering the building.

No attempts had been made to hide him. This killer wanted their handiwork seen. They'd wanted a reaction.

Despite his years working homicide, Ronan's partner gave them one. He and Ronan were different that way.

"Christ," Zach spat out as he took in the condition of the

body and swore again, this time more liberally and with a few words Ronan was sure he'd made up on the spot.

Ronan agreed with the sentiment, knowing this was one of those scenes that would stick with him and show up when he slept, even years from now. Instead of wasting words or trying to block anything out, he dove in, pulling out a small red notebook and silver pen to document the scene.

They would get video and detailed reports from the crime scene technicians who were already on scene, but he liked to have his own impressions from the start. He and Zach would use them as the case bore on, referring back as they filled in the story of their victim's last hours and days.

Death hadn't been easy on the man. He lay on one side, arms and legs splayed and twisted in the kind of position that said at a glance his body was broken beyond repair. There was bruising on his face that didn't fit with the fall. They fit with a fist. He'd gone through a lot before connecting with the concrete that killed him.

Gray duct tape covered the lower half of his face and extended to the back of his head where it wrapped around several times, telling them this killer had wanted to keep him quiet.

Ronan knew the man would have tried to scream all the same and struggled even more, knowing his cries weren't going to bring help.

His clothes were soiled and his hair stringy with dried perspiration and dirt, accounting for some of the smell. The lack of wear on the bottom of the brown leather dress shoes said they were new and the clothes he wore meant this wasn't someone who lived on the streets. Ronan would bet this man came into the building in custom-tailored clothing with clean hair.

"Really?" Zach shook his head at Ronan, going through a familiar refrain that had begun at the first crime scene they'd worked together. "That's it?"

Ronan offered his version of a smile, though people told him he wasn't doing it right. Something about involving more than one corner of his mouth.

Crime scenes bothered him as much as they bothered his partner. The gore, the horror of a life taken, the loss for remaining loved ones. But that didn't mean he needed to go spewing his reaction all over the place.

Zach, on the other end, was a hothead who often ended up counting to one hundred in the bathroom until he cooled himself off when they were working a tough case. When he saw someone lying dead on the ground, he didn't bother to hide what he was thinking and today was no exception.

Dr. Mary Kane, salt-and-pepper hair cut short enough to keep it well out of her way, hovered over the victim, muttering details for her assistant to record. As the lead medical examiner for their jurisdiction, she was a fixture when a death scene told them in plain terms that the death was a homicide, as this one did.

The expressions on the trio of uniformed officers—the more experienced female and the two younger males—standing on the other side of the dead body told Ronan several things. First, the youngest of the two men hadn't handled the scene all that well and was still wearing the pasty skin and cold sweat of someone who had never seen a violent homicide up close.

Second, the older of the two men hadn't fared much better but he was the kind of guy to try to cover his reaction with cocky bravado.

Third, that cocky bravado was aimed at Ronan.

It wasn't unexpected. There was a group of younger officers who had gotten it into their thick heads that betting on what would make Ronan's façade crack was a fun way to pass the time around the station. This guy clearly thought he had a winner with the tableau in front of them.

Ronan watched as the man's face went from confident to confused to annoyed. It wasn't a surprise when he pulled a twenty from his wallet and smacked it into the open palm of the solid brunette woman standing next to him.

Kelly Krantz, a veteran twenty-nine years with the force, pocketed the money with a grin before sending her two cohorts outside to back up the officers serving as gatekeepers against the growing audience.

She threatened to retire weekly, but never did. She didn't take crap from anyone and so far as Ronan knew had never had any designs on making detective or moving up in the chain of command. She was a beat cop through and through, covering a territory on the east side that didn't coddle its inhabitants or the people who policed it.

It was the territory they stood in now, an old neighborhood that was beginning to see some gentrification, which meant people who'd lived here for the cheap rent were being pushed out in increasing numbers as investors tried to cash in on the next *in* place to live.

Ronan ignored the money that had just changed hands, but Zach laughed.

"You didn't tell them Stoney was responding?"

"Why would I do that?" Kelly answered with a wink that made the scar on her left temple crinkle.

She let her grin drop when she moved to shift their focus to the body on the floor. "Security guard retained by the company stopped by to do a routine check on the property and had the misfortune of stumbling on this guy."

Ronan hadn't seen anyone who wasn't with the department but he did a quick scan of the space again. "Where is he now?"

"Tripped and fell in his scramble to get out of here when he saw the body. Hit his head pretty hard on a chunk of concrete."

She gestured to the half of the room that had been gutted down to the studs and the large pile of debris that decorated the area near the back entrance. "My partner took him to the emergency room."

"Yale New Haven?" Ronan asked, noting the information in crisp block letters.

Kelly nodded. "I've got his contact information for you." She reached into the front zipper pocket of her vest and pulled out her phone, turning the screen to allow Ronan to copy the details, before continuing. "He didn't have much to say. Only that he came through to check on the place twice a week and found this."

"Where is the construction crew?" Zach asked in response to the evidence of work in progress around the space.

"Gone. According to the security guard, the job's on hold while they wait for the right materials."

Ronan knew what she meant. He'd been struggling to find any lumber and drywall cheap enough to suit his needs as he attempted to repair a wall and some of the flooring at the nonprofit he volunteered with. A pipe that should have been replaced decades ago had made a mess of the place and Ronan ended up having to pay far more than he'd wanted to for the materials when he realized the situation was going to be the same no matter how far outside of the city he attempted to shop.

Kelly checked her phone for her notes. "The guard said

they stopped work two weeks ago and his company was hired to do regular checks on the site, mostly to make sure vandals or vagrants didn't set up in here."

"When was the last time he came through?" Ronan asked.

"Thursday. He or someone else comes through every Thursday and Monday."

"Nice and regular," Zach said, frustration weighting his tone. A security company ought to know setting up such a rigid routine welcomed trouble.

"Any ID on the victim?" Ronan asked, feeling his own disgust at the company. Their killer had probably known precisely how long he had with the victim before someone would be coming through to check on things.

So long as the heavy tape over his victim's mouth kept things relatively quiet, he'd been able to take his time.

Kelly shook her head. "No wallet or ID in the pockets and the security guard said he didn't know the man."

"Appreciate it," Ronan said as Kelly left and Dr. Kane approached them, her assistant following a few paces behind. The woman barely came to his shoulder, but she was strong and damn good at her job. She was well-liked on the force and, so far as he could tell, in her office.

"Anything noteworthy on this one, Doc?" Ronan dead-panned. And people said he wasn't funny.

Dr. Kane didn't disappoint. "Despite appearances, our victim didn't die from the fall. Come take a closer look," she said, leading them over for a better view. She used gloved hands to roll the still-stiff body to the side so they could see the neck more clearly.

With the shift in position, Ronan could see an angry knife wound that ran down one side of the neck from behind the ear to under the chin. "Looks pretty jagged."

Dr. Kane nodded. "Someone used a dull knife and a lot of strength to cut that deeply. And they did it *before* tossing him off the edge of one of the upper floors." She gestured around. "There isn't enough blood on this floor to be the initial crime scene, but I'm betting you'll find it up there."

Ronan, Zach, and Dr. Kane all looked up, examining the floors above.

"That's not all," the medical examiner said. "There's evidence of significant torture. Take a look at his hands. See the bruising? Someone broke those bones before he died."

She pointed to the fingers and then the blood that marred his arms and stained the clothing around the neck and chest. "Bled before he died."

She stood and removed her gloves, turning them inside out and placing them into a paper bag her assistant provided. "I'll have more for you at the lab."

"Sounds good. In the meantime," Ronan looked toward Zach as he returned his notepad to his back pocket, "let's check out the upper levels."

Ronan understood when his partner cast a wary gaze around them, his eyes landing on the elevator to the far right. It was obviously out of order, with wires sticking out from the spaces where the buttons to call it to the floor should have been.

Zach had recovered physically from their last case when he'd fallen on his head and lost consciousness carrying the officer Zach was now dating down a hidden stone stairwell of an old house. But Ronan had seen the hesitation in Zach's eyes when he had to deal with heights. He would climb when he had to, but he didn't like it.

Ronan looked toward the stairs on the side of the space that didn't seem to have been touched by any demolition tools yet. "The stairs are probably fine, but I can go alone if you want."

"Fuck you," Zach grumbled, leading the way.

Though the stairs were located on the sturdier half of the building, they were just as dusty and filthy as everything else, but it was clear someone had been up and down them several times.

They waited as a forensic technician finished marking and photographing the footprints before taking the stairs themselves.

They didn't need to open the door to the second floor to know the killer hadn't been in there. The heavy layer of grime was untouched.

The same was true of the third floor. They'd have those spaces checked for evidence just in case later, but for now, they continued up.

"Holy hell." Zach coughed when they reached the top floor.

Ronan had to agree. The stench was overwhelming and no amount of mentholated salve was going to help. A sickening combination of rotting blood, urine, and feces. It had been partially responsible for what they'd been smelling on the main floor, but up close it was rancid and foul.

Ronan scanned the floor, spotting a bucket in the corner where flies had gathered, buzzing above it and landing on the edge—a makeshift toilet.

The victim had obviously been held here for more than a few hours.

In the middle of the floor, a wooden chair with an upholstered seat like you might see in the guest position in front of a desk lay on its side, remnants of duct tape stuck to it from where the victim had been bound. The seat of the chair was stained, making it clear the victim had not always been permitted to use the bucket in the corner. Maybe he'd tried to bolt and lost the privilege.

Not far from the chair was the edge where the floor had been cut away during construction. It would have been easy for their killer to free the body from the chair and drag it to the edge to toss over once he slit the victim's throat.

"What are your guesses?" Zach asked, his eyes scanning the scenery in front of them.

"Our buddy downstairs was being held captive here for a while. Then things took a turn for the worst."

"Worse than being held captive and tortured in the first place?"

Ronan frowned. "Exactly. Whoever was holding him here got pissed off about something and cut him then threw him over that edge. I would say our victim must have said something out of line, but his mouth was taped up..."

"Maybe he tried to fight back on the way to the bucket?" Zach offered.

Ronan shook his head and pointed to the area around the chair. "That amount of blood means his throat was slit there, and there's urine and feces on the chair as well. If he did fight back at the bucket, he was bound again after that."

"True." Zach rubbed his chin. "Though maybe the killer just knew his time with the victim was up. With the security company sticking to such a strict routine, he probably knew exactly how much time he had. Which begs the question— if dude had already been tortured and killed, what was the point of cutting him loose and tossing him?"

Zach looked over the edge from a healthy distance. "Maybe we've got ourselves a killer who's into drama. Thought falling from the top floor would add a nice flare. Or hell, maybe it was just a fit of rage."

Ronan nodded his head slowly as the crime scene techs arrived on the top floor.

"Ready for us up here?" one of them asked.

Ronan eyed the edge of the floor where it cut off into a nasty drop. "No. Put in a call to the fire department and ask them to clear this structurally before you gather evidence." He didn't want anyone else taking a potentially deadly fall on his watch.

When the technician nodded, he turned to Zach. "Let's try to get an ID on the victim."

They didn't get more than a foot out of the building before the owner showed up. He was one of those men who shouted and got red in the face first and asked questions later.

When he saw the taped-off building, he chose the closest officer and lit into him.

"You can't do this! Take this down!"

Another of the officers stepped closer, hand on his Taser at his belt. "You need to step back. Now."

"I'm not going anywhere. This is my livelihood. You can't just shut me down." The owner jabbed a finger at the building as he spoke.

Ronan knew what would play out if this continued. They didn't have time for the man to assault one of the officers and then wait on him to be processed into booking before questioning him.

As the owner snatched for the yellow tape, Ronan stepped in. Literally.

He placed himself between the officers and the tall, thin man, offering his card. "Sir, I'm detective Ronan Cafferty. This is my partner, Zach Reynolds. I'm happy to explain what's happened if you'd like to step over here."

He kept his face neutral and gestured with his arm toward the side of the building.

The man grew redder and didn't move. "I don't need an explanation. I need you out of here!"

Ronan spoke again as a news van pulled up, keeping his voice steady and low. "We're really going to be better off moving this elsewhere. Why don't we go around the back of the building where we can talk about this privately?"

The man looked back over his shoulder, blanching as a second news crew arrived.

As the owner acquiesced, Ronan steered him around the back of the building while Zach told the uniformed officer to call for more officers to keep the press at bay.

When they rounded the side of the building, the owner took several deep breaths. Ronan recognized them as the kind of breaths you were taught to take when your temper got the best of you. Inhale through the nose, out through the mouth, nice and slow.

"You're the owner of the building?" Zach asked as Ronan took notes.

The man gave a jerky nod and then offered his name. "Greg Giles. Giles Real Estate."

"You're a real estate agent?" Zach pressed.

"Yeah. I buy commercial properties and fix them up to lease or resell." He looked around. "At least I did before all this supply chain stuff started happening. I'm overextended on properties, and I can't show them until I get them fixed up. My contractor told me he's ready to start working again today, but then I got a call from you guys."

Ronan understood the man's frustration on that end, but the guy didn't seem to get what was going on here. That or he just didn't care, which in Ronan's book spoke volumes about the kind of person he was.

"Did the officer you spoke with on the phone explain what's happened?" Zach asked.

"Yeah, but I can't be responsible for someone going in there and getting hurt. I have signs up all over...and the fence." He gestured at the temporary chain-link fencing around the property.

Something told Ronan this guy had picked the cheapest security company and the cheapest fencing company he could find. There were more than a few places where the panels of fencing weren't properly connected to one another. It would be easy for anyone to pull the panels apart and close them again after accessing the site.

Zach and Ronan shared a glance before Ronan explained. "This wasn't a case of someone walking into your site and dying accidentally." Though with the way half the place had been gutted, that certainly could have happened.

Zach picked up. "We're dealing with a homicide. Someone was killed inside your building."

"Killed? You mean..." He didn't finish as his eyes went to the back door of the building.

Sweat stained the armpits of the man's white collared shirt and he tugged at his tie, loosening the knot before looking around hopelessly again.

He'd gone from angry to dejected in a heartbeat and Ronan might have felt bad for him if he wasn't showing more concern for his wallet than for the life lost in one of his buildings.

"Who has access to this building besides you?" Zach asked.

The man ran his hands up and down his cheeks and blew out a breath. "Uh, me. And my secretary has a key to all of my properties in case she has to show one if I'm not around. And the contractor." He looked up at the sky. "The security company."

When there was a pause, Ronan asked. "Is that it?"

The man gave a nod. "I think so."

Ronan knew the forensics team would check the doors and windows to see how their perpetrator gained access.

Zach pulled his phone from his pocket and brought up one of the photos they'd taken of their victim's face. It wasn't pretty but it was one of the cleaner shots they had.

"Do you recognize this man?" he asked, turning the phone toward Greg.

Greg cursed and began shaking his head in rapid jerks, like he might be able to undo the last few minutes.

"Do you know him?" Ronan prompted.

"No," he said, rubbing his cheeks again. "No, I don't. I'm sorry."

"Who else knew construction had stopped on the building?" Ronan asked.

"The same list as the key, I think." He seemed to think about it for a minute and then nodded. "That's it. When will I have my building back?" He swallowed hard and looked back toward the building. "And who takes care of this all? I mean, you'll take the body and all but is there…"

Ronan took pity on the man and answered without him spelling it out. "Once we release the scene, which might take a few days, there are professional crime scene companies you can hire. They'll know how to handle the cleanup safely and properly."

Greg's shoulders drooped, but he nodded and seemed to accept his fate. They gave him an escort back to his car, complete with all the "no comments" needed to fend off the press before going to their own vehicle.

Just as he and Zach buckled up, Ronan's phone buzzed.

Seeing an incoming call from their captain, he placed the phone on speaker.

For the most part, Captain Calhoun was respected in the major crimes division by all the detectives under him. Ronan was no exception to that rule. Zach liked the captain, too, though he chafed under the man's "swear and you pay up a dollar toward the unit's holiday party" rule.

Ronan was somewhat partial to the cursing kid as far as words went, too, but he was better at keeping them from passing his lips at inopportune times. And that meant whenever the captain was anywhere within earshot since the man seemed capable of hearing them from a distance no matter the task he was occupied with at the time.

"Gentlemen," came the captain's commanding voice, "turns out I likely have an ID on your deceased."

Ronan let out a curse in his head. If the captain was calling with their dead body's ID, the case wasn't going to be a quiet one. Someone of some notoriety was involved.

CHAPTER 2

TWENTY MINUTES LATER, RONAN IGNORED THE FRIED BUTTER smell of an egg-and-bacon breakfast sandwich that filled the cramped space of the captain's office. He and Zach were wedged between matching gray filing cabinets that sported splotches of rust and the back of Captain Calhoun's creaky leather chair, looking over his shoulder at an aging desktop monitor.

The captain wiped his hands on a napkin that matched the pale white of his freckled skin before clicking open a photo that filled the screen.

Ronan leaned closer and examined the image of a middle-aged white man with dirty blond hair posed in a navy suit that matched the dark blue of his eyes. He stood in the sun on the steps of a downtown white stone office building, one foot casually resting on a step a couple above the other.

The man wore the confident smile of someone who knew he'd won the genetics lottery with his broad tanned face and perfect teeth. He leaned against an iron stair railing in a posture meant to tell the viewer he was comfortable in his skin.

He filled out the suit coat well, though he wasn't overly muscular as though he didn't spend hours in the gym to stay fit. Maybe he ran or played squash or tennis at a fancy club to keep in shape.

It was the kind of image you'd see on a professional website, one that promised this was the person you wanted handling whatever problem you'd come to him for, whether that was financial or legal. Possibly medicine, but he wasn't posing in front of a hospital or in a doctor's coat.

Ronan would guess there was a marketing company of some stature running everything in the background.

He refocused on the man's face. The deceased at the center of their investigation had been badly beaten by the time Ronan and Zach laid eyes on him. Still, there was no mistaking the clean-cut man in the photo and the murder victim in that crumbling East New Haven building were one and the same.

"Yeah, that's him." Ronan stepped back, moving toward the chairs on the other side of the desk, his stomach growling at him to remind him that he'd skipped breakfast and needed to make up for it at lunch, and soon. "Or what used to be him."

Zach nodded in agreement, coming around to sit next to Ronan. "We'll get dental records to confirm it. With the state the body's in, no next of kin should have to see it. I'm guessing from how quickly he was identified, this will be a fun one?"

If the captain was involved, he was some kind of bigwig. That was never a good thing. It meant pressure to close the case fast. It meant attention from the press. It meant headaches to add to an already difficult job.

Captain Calhoun folded up the leftover wrap from his breakfast sandwich and tossed it toward a garbage can in the corner. He paused to rub the corner of one eyebrow. "My doctor tells me I have to give up greasy food, but I'm not there yet."

Ronan grinned. The captain had the appetite of a dumpster, tossing down all kinds of fried and salty foods with no concern for how full the receptacle was getting throughout the day. You wouldn't know it from his tall frame, other than a slight bulge he'd sported in the middle for the last decade. Ronan knew from experience, though, that what was happening on the inside of the body didn't always reflect on the outside.

Calhoun leaned back in his seat, the creases around his eyes burrowing deeper as he squinted and gestured to the photo. "Noah Barrett. Age fifty-eight. Lawyer. His law firm handles a lot of big-name clients, including the mayor. The firm's managing partner, Finn Leland, was the one who called the police to report him missing, but the mayor called me personally shortly after to be sure I was aware of the case. I realized pretty quickly he might be yours."

Ronan recorded the information one block letter at a time, not looking up when he spoke. "Why do these names sound so familiar?"

"Because of the law firm," Captain Calhoun answered. "Cartwright, Barrett, and Leland. Pretty prominent place."

Zach snapped his fingers even though it had been Ronan who asked. "That's it," Zach said.

"Even though he wasn't reported missing until today," the captain said, "he's been missing for three days. He didn't show up for a court appearance on Friday, which apparently is highly unusual for him. One of the firm's associates went to Barrett's house. When Barrett wasn't home, they assumed he'd had some kind of emergency, and maybe left town without telling anyone. When there was still no word from him today, Leland decided to report him missing."

"Any family to contact?" Ronan asked, wondering why no one else in their victim's life had reported him missing or why the law firm hadn't followed up over the weekend.

"He's got three adult children, but he's a widower and lived alone." Captain Calhoun shuffled for a file on his desk. "The kids were alerted about their father being reported missing. Contact them and let them know we might have found his body, so they don't see it on the news first."

Ronan frowned. "The press was on the scene when we left."

The captain nodded. "In that case, I'll reach out to the mayor and children personally while we wait for dental records to confirm the ID. You start working the case. The mayor's going to want this resolved quickly and quietly."

It hadn't needed to be said, but there it was. Along with the clock that always ticked over a homicide case as evidence, memories, and leads went stale, they now had an artificial one to up the ante.

The captain handed Zach a thin file. "This is what we've got from the uniform who handled the missing person report this morning. See if there's anything useful in it."

Ronan and Zach headed for their desks in the large bullpen that sat outside the captain's office, taking up a good two-thirds of the space allotted them on the fourth floor of New Haven's main precinct. The room boasted four rows of two desks, each facing the other, so that partners could easily communicate and work together. The rows were six desks long with a break four feet across between the third and fourth desks to allow people to move through the room.

As soon as Ronan settled across from Zach, he opened

his drawer and reached for one of the nut-and-seed granola bars he kept there. It was going to have to do for breakfast and likely lunch today. Screw it. He pulled two from the box and bit off half of one as he took the first sheet of the report from Zach, who had already scanned it.

Zach continued to pass the pages to Ronan but there wasn't much for either of them to read.

"Is it just me, or is there nothing particularly helpful in this?" Ronan asked when he'd finished the last page.

Zach had been watching Ronan read and added his agreement. "Not just you. It's skin and bones but then they only had a few hours before Calhoun pulled it for us to handle."

A missing person report was always taken by a uniformed officer on the first floor of the building where officers rotated in and out on a schedule between patrol shifts. They would follow up, collecting information before passing it up to a detective if they found anything to suggest the person was the victim of foul play.

There was a separate unit that handled runaway kids, of which there were sadly too many for major crimes to take.

Ronan turned back to the beginning of the report and read through the pages again to ensure neither of them had somehow overlooked useful information. As he did, he wrote notes to supplement what he'd written in the captain's office.

None of Noah Barrett's neighbors had seen anything or noticed anything unusual with him prior to his disappearance. He was known for leaving the house early and returning late. Some reported that when his wife had been alive, they hosted holiday parties for friends, but since her passing the parties stopped. With his wife gone and his kids grown and living out of state, he rarely had visitors anymore.

Poor bastard. Any connection he had to people or community seemed to have died right along with his wife. Ronan's own social life wasn't anything to get excited about, but damn he liked to think his neighbors and friends would have more to offer than this.

Come to think of it, though, it would probably have to be his partner or someone at the tutoring center where he volunteered to call attention to his absence if he went missing. There wasn't a girlfriend or a sports team or something like that to notice.

"Knock, knock." The voice drew Zach and Ronan's attention, but Zach's more than Ronan's since it belonged to Zach's woman.

Ronan looked up to see Shauna O'Rourke standing over their desks, a sappy smile on her face as she looked at Zach.

Zach was looking at her the same way, like they hadn't just seen each other a few hours ago when they woke up together.

They might be all eyes on each other, but Ronan was looking at the raven-haired woman standing next to Shauna.

The Irish heritage of both women was plain, but where Shauna was lean and long with strawberry blonde hair, the woman with her had dark Irish looks and a curvy frame that worked well with her shorter height.

The woman's dark hair was a contrast to her fair freckled skin and hazel eyes, but the combination was intriguing. And when she smiled, her eyes danced with light, stopping Ronan cold.

No, cold wasn't right. He was doused with heat at the sight of the woman, not a reaction he was used to having from nothing more than a look. Yes, he'd spot a hot woman in a bar and be interested enough to approach and maybe take her home for the night, but it wasn't anything like this.

It wasn't an instant awareness of every curve of her body, of the way her smile was slightly crooked, making it all the more appealing.

It wasn't the kind of head-to-toe burning that pushed him to find out more. To make sure he knew who she was and how to find her again before she walked away.

She was stunning.

Shauna cleared her throat, pulling Ronan's gaze from the mystery woman with a quirked brow that said she hadn't missed his interest in her friend. He didn't care.

Shauna stood with one hip cocked toward Zach, letting her arm touch his arm. Ronan had noticed they did that a lot. They were always professional, but they managed a slight contact here or there. "Gentlemen, this is Tiff Carson. Tiff, this is my Zach."

Zach nodded politely.

Shauna raised her hand to gesture to Ronan. "And this guy is Detective Ronan Cafferty. He's the man who has my man's back out on the streets."

Shauna could have introduced him as the king for all Ronan cared in that moment. His focus was on Tiff Carson. He had a name now.

Tiff smiled, her hazel eyes sparkling. "Nice meeting you both." Tucking the notebook she carried under her arm, she shook Zach's hand before extending a hand to Ronan.

Ronan's eyes dropped to scan the rest of her again as he shook her hand.

The hell, man. Don't be a creep. With some difficulty, he focused on her face again.

That wasn't a hardship. One of her eyes was more green than hazel, but only by a hair, something he hadn't noticed before. He liked it. She wasn't perfect, and yet, she somehow was.

"I brought Tiff here to speak to you guys. She researches cold cases and has been examining the Herschel Kenworth case."

The name Herschel Kenworth was one every detective in the unit knew well. A year ago, there'd been a string of murders in New Haven, eerily reminiscent of murders that had taken place thirty years prior, dubbed by the press at the time as the Marsh Killer since the killer had dumped one of the bodies in a marsh.

After a lot of time and frustration—not to mention a much-too-close call for both Shauna and Zach—they'd revealed the killer to be Liz Gordon, the niece of Herschel Kenworth, who they now knew was the original Marsh Killer. In the aftermath, she was convicted of multiple first-degree homicides.

Kenworth was long dead, so there was no justice for the families of his victims and, without knowing why he'd killed the girls or much about what had happened, there wasn't a whole lot of closure either. At least not as much as they'd like to give the families in a case like that.

"Tiff has interviewed me, of course, and she's looking into people who knew Herschel, but she's also hoping to interview you to see if she can piece together more of what happened. Your captain's given you permission to discuss it with her, so long as you stick to the facts of the Kenworth case and don't go too deeply into Liz Gordon's."

Ronan nodded and leaned forward in his chair. "Liz Gordon's case is still under appeal so we aren't at liberty to speak from that angle much, but we're definitely happy to share what we can."

Tiffany met the eye of the handsome detective. "I appreciate it."

She hadn't missed the way he'd been eyeing her, and she didn't mind eyeing him back. He had dark, silky hair she wanted to reach out and touch, picturing tugging on it in bed as he... she caught herself and stopped the thought. Damn.

It wasn't her fault. Ronan Cafferty had a physique designed to make grown women drool. The epitome of tall, dark, and handsome, with what seemed to be naturally tanned skin, dark brown eyes, and a no-nonsense way about him that was sexy as hell.

Shauna hadn't mentioned her boyfriend's partner was a drop-dead hottie. Then again, Shauna might have given up on the idea of Tiff dating. It had been a while.

If a while meant years, that is. Tiff's focus was on her career and making tenure. Not to mention she'd figured out a long time ago that men weren't into smart women. For a while, she'd gone on a dating site using a fake career and profile and pretending to be a lot more interested in fashion and makeup than history and criminology, but that was only useful to scratch an occasional itch. You couldn't build a relationship on a lie and she got bored with the men she met on those sites in a matter of a few dates.

She didn't date anyone at work. That either ended with them being upset if she threatened their position in any way —or they perceived her as threatening it. Or with them being pompous asses who tried to mansplain anything and everything to her without acknowledging that she had a brain as big as or bigger than theirs.

So, yeah, Shauna had probably assumed Tiff was firmly entrenched in her commitment to celibacy.

But damn, if there was ever a man to pull her out of it, this was him.

"Are you researching the case for fun or for work?" Ronan asked.

Screeech. Tiff could hear the brakes squeal as her fantasy jerked to a halt. No way to answer that question without letting Hottie McCop know exactly who she was. So much for scratching any itch on that post.

Most people found what she did morbid at best and at the very least, creepy, which meant she was a double whammy. Smart and creepy.

She shook her head, plastering on the smile she normally reserved for big donors to her department at the fundraising events academia required. "I'm a history professor at a nearby college with a focus in criminal history."

"Yeah, probably should have mentioned that first," Shauna said, laughing. She patted Tiff on the shoulder. "Didn't mean to make you look like a weirdo who does this for giggles."

"No worries. It's not like I'm unfamiliar with people thinking I'm a weirdo," Tiff said, seeing Ronan's reaction play out like clockwork.

One minute, he'd been checking her out and the next, he'd tossed up a metaphorical No Trespassing sign. He kept a polite façade on his face, but that's all it was. The intensity and heat were gone.

"So, you guys aren't going to have a problem with Tiff hanging around and conducting her research? As long as the Liz-related stuff is left out?" Shauna asked.

Ronan shrugged his shoulders, looking at Shauna instead of Tiff when he answered. "I guess that's all right."

Tiff cleared her throat and threw back her shoulders, wrapping herself in a protective sheen of *I don't give a crap*. It had been a fun little foray into la-la land, but she was back to reality now.

"I won't push for information you can't disclose. I know the rules and I respect the boundaries." She set her folder down on the edge of Zach's desk, opened it, and pulled out an envelope tucked between its pages. "But I was hoping you could confirm that a few old pictures that I found of Herschel Kenworth and his family members are really him." Tiff handed the photos over, passing some to Zach and some to Ronan. "Shauna has confirmed it, but I try to have more than one source document anything that's going into my work."

She could see Zach was familiar with the Kenworth family, judging from the grimace on his face as he viewed the photos. Ronan barely moved what had become a granite veneer as he looked at them.

Annoyance flared in her chest. He didn't have to be that much of a dick.

"Yeah, that's them." Zach shook his head. "If there ever was an argument for nature over nurture, this family is it."

"I've reached out to the family for interviews," Tiff said, "but of course, most of them refuse to talk. I've been able to speak to a few friends of the family, but their knowledge is pretty limited. I'd like to interview the two of you and find out as much as you're willing to tell."

"We're happy to help when we can," Ronan prefaced, handing the photos back to her, "but we're busy at the moment with a new case. If you want to talk, it's going to have to be at a later date."

Tiff felt her cheeks heat as she took the photos and returned them to the envelope. "I understand."

She offered a brittle smile and wondered why she cared so much that this man was acting this way. It was no matter to her that he wasn't falling over himself to make her feel welcome. She was here to do a job and nothing more.

Besides, his boss had already given her clearance. It wasn't like Ronan could say no to her now.

But he can avoid a sit-down and make this much more difficult than it needs to be, she reminded herself.

"How about we get in touch day after tomorrow, once things have settled down some?" Zach said, softening his partner's bluntness.

Maybe she could have Shauna and Zach over for dinner and get what she needed from them. She'd already talked to one of the other detectives in Shauna's cold case unit. Maybe she could bypass Hottie McCop altogether.

"Great," Tiff said, that fake smile in place again. "I'll be in touch then."

As she walked away, she tried to tell herself he didn't look very hot anymore, but that was a lie. The stone mountain impression he'd been doing should have made him look worse, but it hadn't. Instead, he had that brooding thing going for him.

Damn it, she wasn't the kind of woman to fall for that kind of crap. Not at all. She jammed the elevator button as she worked to convince herself of that little lie.

CHAPTER 3

Ronan shoved hard at his mind and forced all thoughts of the woman down deep. The long black hair that would probably feel like silk in his hands. The eyes that would burn with heat when he got her naked. Those curves he wanted to sink into. None of it mattered.

He didn't do teachers. Ever.

That locked-away place inside him that said this might be different struggled up to the top and opened its mouth, ready to argue. He punched it back down, beating it into submission where it belonged and began adding more reasons to stay away from Tiff Carson on top of it. The more buried those thoughts were, the better.

Getting in bed with a good friend of his partner's someday wife was a piss-poor idea to begin with.

She wasn't even *just* a teacher. She was a college professor. Whole new level of *hell no* there.

He looked across to Zach who had finally pulled himself away from his woman. "We better get a move on with this case. Let's pay the victim's law firm a visit. If our killer really did hold Noah Barrett prisoner for three days while he beat him, this isn't a random killing."

Zach stood from his desk and grabbed the keys to their assigned vehicle. "You read my mind. Noah doesn't seem to have much of a personal life. Might as well start with work and see if there's a motive that ties to any of his clients."

Twenty minutes later, the detectives were standing outside of the sleek gray stone office building that housed Cartwright, Barrett, and Leland, Attorneys at Law. The concrete stairs with the iron railing from the photo led up to a wide glass front with double doors at the center.

When they entered the lobby with its vaulted ceiling and marble floor, a petite golden-haired receptionist flashed them a five-star smile that looked a little too white to be natural. "Good afternoon, gentlemen. How can I help you?" She asked this while tossing her long curls over one shoulder.

Ronan and Zach presented their leather-encased badges.

"Detectives Reynolds and Cafferty of the New Haven Police Department," Zach said. "We need to speak with Finn Leland."

"One moment, please." She ran pink polished nails over her keyboard, filling the silence with the click-clack of her nails on the keys. Moments later she graced them with another of those full-watt smiles like they'd won a prize. "I'll show you in."

She walked ahead of them on too-tall heels that once would have had Ronan dreaming about her long legs wrapped around him still in the shoes and nothing else. Or maybe fully dressed. Just her black skirt pushed up and her panties pulled off. Or pulled to the side depending on how much of a rush he was in to be inside her.

Yes, he'd once been the kind of pig who would have all those fantasies and more when he followed a woman down a hallway like this. He wasn't that guy anymore. In fact, until that morning it had been a while since he'd paid much attention to a woman. He'd been too buried in work and his projects at the tutoring center to do much else.

So, he mostly ignored the woman and her heels, except to thank her when she showed them into a large corner office with all the floor-to-ceiling windows and swank polished wood furnishings businesspeople of the world dream about.

Ronan had never aspired to this, but the view out the window was admittedly nice. It looked out over the green at the center of town with its mature elm trees and the traditional stone buildings of the Yale University campus.

He wondered if Tiff Carson worked at Yale. Probably not. She'd said a nearby college. Surely she wouldn't call Yale a nearby college.

The man behind the desk stood, thick black hair perfectly in place and a smile on his face that made small lines appear at the corners of his gray-blue eyes. He was the kind of man who could have been forty or sixty. He was either right on track with the few wrinkles on his face or admirably behind the expected timeline if he was the latter.

"Gentlemen, I've just heard from the mayor. Do you have any leads?" Finn Leland shook each of their hands in turn.

He was dressed in a dark gray suit with a white shirt and a tie that perfectly matched the color of his eyes. Everything about him screamed savvy lawyer, but he was nuts if he thought they'd tell him anything about an ongoing investigation. Ronan didn't like people who thought their position or contacts could get them something they weren't entitled to, and unless this man had earned a police badge on the sly, he wasn't getting anything on their case.

"We're only at the beginning of our inquiries," Ronan said, putting a little more formal into his tone to be sure the man knew they wouldn't be manipulated.

Leland waited a beat too long before trying to brush off Ronan's rebuff. "Sure, sure. I understand. Please, take a seat." He gestured to the wide black leather chairs in front of his desk, before taking his own seat, also black leather.

Ronan pulled out his pen and notepad. "You were the one to call in and report him missing this morning?"

Leland nodded. "Noah never misses work, so I figured something was wrong." His eyes darted from Zach to Ronan. "I only wish I'd called you on Friday instead of assuming he was handling an emergency that precluded a call to us in a timely manner."

"Would he do that?" Zach asked. "Forget to call someone if he wasn't coming to the office?"

Leland's face fell. "No. I should have seen something was wrong. Truth be told, we had a lot going on Friday and we were juggling when we had to step in on his case. My focus was on our client."

His regret seemed genuine to Ronan, but they'd been doing this too long to take someone at face value. They wouldn't immediately discount the fact their victim's firm hadn't called the police earlier.

"When is the last time you talked to Mr. Barrett?" Zach asked.

Leland glanced at the ceiling and narrowed his eyes. "Thursday. I left the office at around eight o'clock that evening. Noah was still here prepping for his court appearance."

"What trial is that?" Ronan asked.

Leland paused, pressing his lips together before speaking. "I suppose it's public information. He was lead counsel on the Whitworth defense team."

That was unexpected. Zach sat forward in his chair. Ronan didn't.

Archer Whitworth was a state representative who'd been arrested for manslaughter when he'd driven his car off the side of the highway after a night of drinking. He plowed into a teenager and left her for dead, driving away and going home to his bed.

The teen, an honor student from a family without the means to pay for college, had earned a full ride in scholarships to a prestigious university, but because of Whitworth, she died on the side of the road alone. Her body wasn't discovered until the morning, and even then most of the morning commuters drove right by the ditch she'd been lying in.

It was only after a trucker saw her from his elevated position that she was found.

Once Whitworth was identified as the driver, it was seen as a case of a wealthy, prominent man with a complete lack of regard for anyone beneath him. Community protests began right away, but Ronan was proud to say they hadn't been needed to start the wheels of justice rolling in this case. The New Haven Police Department arrested him and the prosecutor's office wasn't holding back in their prosecution of the crime.

The list of people who might want to sabotage Archer Whitworth's defense was long. They'd have to find out if any of those people might be angry enough to torture and kill the man defending him.

Ronan made a note to look at why someone would target the lawyer but not Whitworth himself.

"Did your partner's absence affect the Whitworth case?" Zach asked, and Ronan knew he was exploring potential motivations for the murder. He'd been thinking the same thing.

"Not at all," Leland said, sounding insulted. "There were several associates helping Noah on the case and I'm familiar enough with the court filings and progress in the case that I was able to get up to speed quickly and step in."

Ronan wasn't so sure that would make a difference. Would an outsider know that, or would they think going after the lawyer might make a difference in Whitworth's conviction?

"So you were busy with the case on Friday? Did you try contacting Mr. Bartlett over the weekend to check in with him?" Ronan asked.

Leland's jaw tightened. "No, I'm afraid I didn't. I had some personal things happening over the weekend..."

"Such as..." Ronan pushed.

The jaw began to tick, a slight muscle reaction Leland wouldn't know how to control.

He answered, though. "My wife and I had a falling out. I went to stay on my brother's couch."

Ronan didn't let him off. "You didn't think to have someone here call the police? You sent an associate to his house. You didn't think that maybe you should call the police when he didn't find Mr. Barrett home?"

Leland had already answered the question, but Ronan wanted to hear it again. They often asked things in several ways to be sure a witness didn't change their story.

Mr. Leland had to know what Ronan was doing, but he shifted in his seat before answering. "I wasn't going to call the police just because a grown man missed one day of work. Like I said, I thought he had a family emergency or something. You can't tell me it's customary for someone to call the police on their coworker for missing work. Come on, give me a break."

"But it was concerning to you the first time he missed work, right?" Zach said.

"Yeah. But what was I supposed to do? I didn't want to risk making a false report if he happened to show up later, perfectly fine."

"But just to reiterate, missing work is something you've never known Mr. Barrett to do?" Ronan said. "Didn't that seem off to you?"

Mr. Leland grimaced, no longer able to hide his irritation at the circular questioning. "No. But in life, you can never say never, can you? And again, as I've expressed to you gentlemen, it didn't strike me as appropriate to call the police on my colleague just because he didn't show up to work for the first time. Yes, it was unusual. But Noah's a grown man. If something was wrong, he should have called."

Ronan could see regret under the façade the man was putting on for them.

"Thank you, Mr. Leland," Ronan said. He and Zach exchanged quick glances, recognizing that they had gotten under Mr. Leland's skin—precisely what they needed to do. Frustration often made people less guarded. And being less guarded meant being more truthful, even if by accident.

There was a fine line not to cross though. Frustrating an interviewee too much could cause them to shut down and become uncooperative.

Or call the mayor they had connections with. They didn't want that so early on in the case.

In Ronan's eight years of being a detective, it was a dance he had learned to do well.

"Are we finished here?" Mr. Leland asked impatiently.

"Just about." Zach smiled now and softened things again. "Can you think of anything else that might cause someone to target Mr. Barrett? Maybe a case someone was angry about? Information someone might have wanted to get out of him?"

"*What*?" Leland's eyes darted from one detective to the other, his face paling on the spot. "What exactly happened to Noah?"

Ronan weighed how much to say before going with a vague answer. "Mr. Barrett may have been beaten before he was killed."

"Shit." Leland ran a hand over his bald head and leaned back in his seat, his agitation gone entirely and replaced with shock. "Why? Who would do that?"

"Precisely what we're trying to figure out," Zach said. "Do you know anyone who was angry with Mr. Barrett?"

"No," Leland answered, dumbfounded.

"Did Mr. Barrett only handle criminal defense law?" Ronan asked with his pen hovering at the ready over his notepad.

Mr. Leland nodded shakily. "Yes. Has for the last twenty-some years. Before that he was a public defender."

Zach leaned forward slightly. "May we see his case files and a list of his clients, please?"

Mr. Leland's eyes went shrewd again. The lawyer was back in control and he shook his head slowly. "That's privileged information. I can't share that with you. But I can assure you there was no one he was working with that would have a vendetta strong enough to kill the poor man."

"We'll get a warrant if we need to," Ronan replied.

"Please do," Mr. Leland said. "Until then, I'm happy to cooperate in any other way you need."

"We'd like to speak to your assistant and the associate who was sent to the house to look for Mr. Barrett," Zach informed.

It only took about ten minutes for Leland to set them up in a conference room with the individuals Zach had requested. After questioning the assistant and not getting any useful information, Ronan and Zach spoke with the associate who had been sent to Mr. Barrett's house, Marcus Jones.

Marcus was five foot eight at most, dressed in a suit and tie that held hints of the 1950s with brown-and-tan wing tipped shoes to match. His black skin was light behind a mustache and neatly trimmed beard, and the confidence he owned when he entered the room was impressive.

Ronan always pictured the young associates of a law firm as scurrying lackies, but this man was anything but that. Then again, he'd landed a job in one the state's most prestigious firms, so maybe he'd earned that confidence legitimately.

"Mr. Jones, it's our understanding that when Mr. Barrett didn't arrive for his trial on Friday, you went by his home to check on him," Zach said.

Jones gave a single nod. His face showed no sign of guile or guards. "That's correct."

"What did you find?"

"Nothing." A shrug rolled through his shoulders. "Everything seemed normal. Like he just hadn't returned home from wherever he'd gone to."

"No signs of struggle?" Ronan asked while taking notes.

A head shake, no, this time.

"Do you know any reason someone would want to hurt Mr. Barrett? Did he have any disputes with anyone that you knew about?"

Jones frowned, bringing his hands to the arms of his chair as he sat forward, face showing he was giving some thought to it instead of just rattling off a pat reassurance that Barrett was a great guy no one would want to hurt.

"None that I can think of. He's well liked even though he pushes people to work hard. If you're working with him, you know you're going to pull all-nighters when it comes time for discovery in a case or prep for a trial or big motion."

"What do you know about his personal life?" Zach asked.

"Can you be more specific?"

"We know he was widowed. But was he dating anyone recently?"

Marcus tipped his head. "Another lawyer in town, I think. I'm not sure how long they'd been together, but I know it was at least a month because she came to last month's company gathering with him."

"Her name?" Ronan asked.

"Yasmine Bray."

Ronan wrote *Yasmine Bray, pot. gf* on his notepad. "Anything else you can think of?"

"No," Marcus said. "Like you said, he was widowed. I think he has kids, but I'm not sure."

They had one thing to go on, though. Apparently, his personal life wasn't as dead as his neighbors thought.

CHAPTER 4

RONAN BREATHED DEEP, INHALING THE SCENT OF FRESH-BAKED rye bread and corned beef, glad for the chance to clear his head of the case for a few minutes as they ate. They'd been just in time to beat the foot traffic that was beginning to get heavy as the office buildings around Noah Barrett's law firm spat out their inhabitants for the lunchtime rush.

In another five minutes, they would have had to wait in a long line for lunch anywhere in the downtown business district. Instead, they were now seated at a too-small table in the back corner of a small deli. Ronan knew they were also just in time to stave off the headache that would have formed if he'd gone much longer without eating.

His partner knew him well and didn't try to talk as Ronan took his first bite of the monster sandwich in front of him. He groaned.

It was several more bites before he attempted civilized conversation. "We need to remember this place," he said around a mouthful of food.

Zach grunted his agreement, working on his own case of food-induced bliss with a pastrami on rye.

When they slowed on the second half of their sand-wiches, Ronan spoke. "Barrett's house first or the girlfriend?"

They had uniformed officers watching the house until the crime scene team could get there so they didn't need to worry that anyone might disturb any evidence that might be there.

Zach sat back, wadding up his napkins in the parchment from his sandwich. "I think we should hit the house and see if that's where Barrett was grabbed from. If we know a time frame and where he was grabbed, we might get more from her."

Ronan nodded, collecting his own trash to throw away. "I wonder what her excuse for not calling the police will be."

"I hope someone raises the alarm a lot faster for me if I'm ever grabbed," Zach said as they stood to get back to work.

Ronan had to agree. He didn't have the most active social life on the planet but he liked to think more than a few people would give a shit if he didn't show up where he should be.

Fifteen minutes later, Ronan looked out the car window as Zach pulled up to Noah Barrett's house. The neighbor-hood was quiet.

Sure, it was Monday and most people were at work, their kids at school, but still, Ronan got the impression it was always a quiet neighborhood, complete with perfect lawns and neighbors who minded their own business. There were no bikes out front of houses or dogs running loose.

A truck was parked on the curb in front of the house across the street, with a metal tool chest bolted across the width of the bed. *Hadley's Handyman and Honey Do* was written on the side in black block lettering with an image of a hammer and drill worked into the lettering.

With the exception of the patrol car parked out front, Barrett's house looked like any other on the street. Tudor brick with soaring gables, copper gutters, and a copper-topped bay window. Meticulously maintained shrubs fronted the home with a cobblestone walk cutting through the thick green of the lawn.

Marcus Jones had been right, at least from the outside. The house seemed undisturbed and there was nothing out of the ordinary to hint at foul play. Patrol officers had checked the house for any other victims as soon as Barrett had been identified, but now they were waiting for a search warrant to enter the home.

With the connections Barrett had, they'd likely have one soon, unless someone tried to stop them getting into the house.

Ronan and Zach got out of the car and checked in with the patrol officer sitting in his car in the driveway before approaching the home. Ronan eyed the doorknob, noting that there were no scratches on the handle or locks. None of the windows looked to be disturbed.

"Let's check out the back," Zach suggested.

The backyard was as impeccably landscaped as the front, with a flagstone patio outside the French doors leading into the house and a freestanding two-car garage at the back of the property.

Ronan took in the neighbors' homes as they walked further into the backyard. Each lot was at least a quarter acre so there was plenty of space between each of the houses. This wasn't the kind of neighborhood where you looked out your bathroom window into your neighbor's.

Would anyone hear Barrett scream for help if he had been grabbed inside?

The sound of a vacuum cleaner started, and Ronan and Zach shared a look. It was plainly coming from the garage on Barrett's property. As they'd been told no one but Barrett lived in the house, they shouldn't be hearing anyone inside. Much less someone cleaning up the place.

Zach and Ronan signaled to one another, pulling their service weapons as they moved. Whoever was inside wouldn't be able to open the overhead doors and go out that way without giving Ronan and Zach time to block them so they both moved to flank the entrance on the right side of the garage.

Ronan's heart rate kicked up as it always did when they were headed into the unknown. He never worried about it. His body's reaction told him he was on guard, as he should be. Ronan was in control, keeping his breathing steady and his eyes and ears alert.

This building should have been swept by the patrol officers when they cleared the house earlier in the day, but clearly it hadn't. Was this their killer cleaning up the scene of the initial crime? Had Barrett been grabbed when he pulled into his garage?

If he had, the killer would have been able to secure Barrett in his trunk and use his own vehicle to drive him right out without anyone realizing anything had happened. Finn Leland had said Barrett was still in the office Thursday evening so it might have been dark by the time he came home. It was the perfect time and opportunity to grab him.

Zach gave a nod and Ronan reached for the door, swinging it wide as he and Zach moved in tandem.

"New Haven Police!" Zach called out over the sound of the vacuum cleaner. "Let me see your hands."

It was evident the fifty-something-year-old man was startled when he dropped the vacuum cleaner and hunched his head, covering it with his hands.

"Don't shoot! Don't shoot!"

Ronan scanned the rest of the large space. From his vantage, he could see it all. There was no car, but one side was empty as though waiting for its occupant to return. The other was cluttered but for the area in front of the shelves where the man had been working.

The man was alone with his vacuum working on a set of empty shelves that ran along one side of the garage. The smell of wood stain hit Ronan at the same time that he took in the tool belt slung low on the man's hips.

He lowered his weapon toward the floor, finger off the trigger but ready. "Can you tell us what you're doing in Noah Barrett's garage?"

Zach shot Ronan a glance before holstering his weapon and stepping farther into the space to shut off the vacuum cleaner, leaving them standing in silence waiting for the man's answer.

His hands shook as he lowered them and Zach saw he had dark brown hair shot through with gray, brown eyes, and the hands of a man who worked with them for a living.

"I'm his contractor. I'm cleaning up. I try to leave a job site clean when I'm finished."

Zach pointed to the wall of the garage. "Put your hands on the wall for me, please, and spread your legs out. You're at an active crime scene. I'm going to check you for weapons. Is there anything in your pockets that could cut me or hurt me in any way?"

The man shook his head as he assumed his stance against the wall.

Zach pulled out a pair of latex gloves and donned them

before beginning a pat down and search of the man's pockets. He removed the hammer hanging from the tool belt and a screwdriver, laying them on one of the shelves before continuing.

When he came to the man's wallet, he set that aside as well and continued his search. When he'd finished, he pointed to an old coffee table stacked among some other cast-off furniture on one side of the garage. "Have a seat for me."

"What is your name, sir?" Zach asked.

Ronan holstered his weapon, but he wasn't ready to relax completely. He didn't take his notepad out. He'd remember these details and write them out when they got back to their vehicle.

"Ted Hadley," the man said, craning his neck to see around them out into the yard. "Has something happened?"

Zach gestured at the man's wallet. "Go ahead and pull out your identification for me, please."

When Hadley had done as Zach asked, producing a Vermont driver's license, Ronan radioed to have the identification confirmed. Moments later, they had their answer. Ted Hadley was legit and had no prior record of anything more than a parking ticket in either Vermont or Connecticut.

The tension in the garage eased a notch and Zach and Ronan turned their attention toward gathering any information the man might have for them.

"You said you're here doing construction for Mr. Barrett. Do you always work when your client isn't home?" Ronan asked.

The man's brow creased, like he didn't understand the question. "I've done work for him a few times over the last year, and I do work for the church Mr. Barrett attends. That's how he found me."

"Did he always let you work on your own while he wasn't home?" Zach asked.

Hadley frowned. "Sure, once he's shown me what he wants and all. This time I already knew because we'd discussed it before so he just called Thursday and said to come by when I could." He gestured toward the shelves. "It was an easy job. I started it on Friday afternoon and finished it up last night, but I was letting the stain dry before I came back to clean up and make sure there weren't any areas that needed another coat."

Hadley looked at the two of them more intently. "Something happened to Mr. Barrett?"

Zach ignored the question. "So you spoke to him via phone Thursday. Did he come by at all when you were working?"

"Not this time. He sometimes comes home when I'm still around in the evening, but he works a lot." He looked in the direction of the house. "Is Mr. Barrett okay? Did something happen?"

Ronan answered, wanting to see the reaction he got. "Mr. Barrett was murdered sometime in the last few days. We're working on piecing together a timeline."

Hadley's eyes went wide and he swore in a whisper that didn't hide the severity of the word.

Quiet hovered over them as Hadley stared at the floor, one hand rubbing the back of his neck as he seemed to attempt to come to grips with the information Ronan had just thrown at him.

Ronan had now pulled out his notepad and began taking notes. "What time were you here on those days?" Ronan asked, filling his notepad with Ted's responses.

"Around three o'clock to seven o'clock or so on Thursday. Sunday afternoon from four to seven. It wasn't a big job so I was fitting it in with other jobs."

"And you didn't hear from Mr. Barrett again any time after Thursday?"

Ted shook his head. "I was going to text him when I finished today and then leave the key in the mailbox. That's what I usually do, then he'll leave a check for me and I'll swing by and grab it out of the box."

"While you were working at the house, did anyone else stop by on either of those days?" Zach asked.

"I don't think so. At least, not that I know of. I was out here with power tools and ear protectors on most of the time, though. If anyone came up to the front of the house, I'm afraid I wouldn't know. I did go inside to use the bathroom a time or two, but I didn't see anyone."

Nothing helpful, Ronan thought. He tucked his pen and notepad back into his pocket. As he was about to thank Ted for his cooperation, another question came to him. "Hey, by any chance, do you still have the key to Mr. Barrett's house?"

"Yeah, I do." He reached into his jeans' pocket and handed the key over before Ronan could even ask for it.

Good. It would come in handy when the warrant on the house came through.

CHAPTER 5

Tiff stopped in the doorway to her office, keys in hand, breathing in the comfort of the space. The scent of books and ink greeted her, and when she trailed closer to her desk there was the cherry tobacco smell of her grandmother coming from the quilted lap throw hanging over the back of the chair.

She ran a hand over the deep burgundy and cream triangles of the quilted pattern, needing the balm it provided. For years, she'd brought the throw home with her on her monthly visits to see her grandmother in Long Island. She would set it in her grandmother's room to soak up the smell so she'd have the most important person in her world with her when she came back to Connecticut.

Somehow in her little girl's mind years ago, she'd assumed her grandmother smelled like cherry tobacco because she packed her grandfather's pipes for him. Never mind the fact she'd never seen her grandfather smoke a pipe in the ten years of her life he'd been alive. It was only some story her mind had invented to assign to the smell.

A year ago, when she'd had to move her grandmother

into a nursing home, she mentioned it to her grandmother. Tiff wasn't sure she'd ever laughed so hard in her life when Gran told her that was the smell of the Boom Boom lotion she used. When Tiff had caught her breath, Gran explained the lotion was a brand of lotion known for keeping cellulite at bay.

That only brought back the giggles and Tiff had been crying by the time Gran rolled up her sleeve, showing off her eighty-eight-year-old bicep to display the results.

Today's visit with her grandmother hadn't had nearly that level of laughter involved. After spending the morning being reminded her intelligence was a turn-off to men—and yes, her heedless mind was still flitting back to Ronan Cafferty's tantalizing physique even hours later—Tiff had gone to see Gran in the home.

Every day was hit or miss lately with Gran's health. Some days, Tiff could convince herself Gran would live forever as she rolled her wheelchair around the rec room, the fingerless bike gloves that protected her hands flashing ruby sequins as she went.

More and more of the time, Tiff found Gran as she had this morning, sleeping so soundly she hadn't stirred in the hour and a half Tiff sat by her bed. Her doctors hadn't found anything wrong with her to explain the fatigue, but Tiff felt more and more like her Gran was slipping away from her and she didn't know how to stop that.

She felt haggard now as she started the electric tea kettle, shifting it so it sat firmly on the hand painted sage green stool by the window. As she waited on the water, she dropped a cinnamon tea bag in a chipped blue mug and then used the repurposed milk jug she kept on the windowsill to give her plants a drink. She only kept the hardiest of plants. The kind that were exceedingly forgiving if she forgot to water them.

She'd found she could keep spider plants alive fairly well, and pothos. She could also take trimmings from them to root and pot, which let her fill Gran's room in the home with plants as well. Gran's home in Long Island had an impressive garden Tiff had never been able to replicate, but she could do her best to make sure there was greenery when Gran wasn't up to getting out of bed.

When the teapot whistled, she poured the hot water over her tea bag before settling in at her desk, ready to look over her latest notes. Her research and the resulting writing to produce something publishable could be laborious, but it was a challenge Tiff thoroughly enjoyed and on a day like today she turned to her work as a distraction.

She felt a special pride in her current project. This one would focus on the history of crimes against women and provide an analysis on the impact such crimes had on women's roles in politics, society, and family.

It would be her best work yet, she was sure.

Before she could get into what she'd hoped would be a solid few hours of alone time to focus, a knock sounded on her door.

She held her breath a minute, wondering if she could ignore it. Given the frosted glass on the top half of her door that let people see forms and shadows in the room, the answer was no, but she toyed with the idea all the same.

"Come in," she relented.

James Atkins's head appeared as he poked it around the door, then entered with a broad smile on his blotchy face.

Tiff couldn't muster even the hint of a smile for him today. Not that she gave him a genuine one on a good day. It was always forced with this man.

In his early fifties, he had thinning black hair and beady gray eyes she found unnerving. Like Tiff, James was a tenured professor of history, though his focus was on Roman history. In his estimation, that made him better than her somehow.

Of course, just because he didn't see her mind as up to par didn't mean he wasn't interested in her body. Almost as long as Tiff had known him, he'd relentlessly tried to get in her pants. The last university she'd worked at had taught her the dangers of dating coworkers and the awkwardness that ensued if the relationship didn't work out.

Oh, and there was the fact he was married. The man was a peach.

"Hey, Tiffany," James said, a slight smirk on his face. Although he didn't ask her out with the same frequency he used to after she'd begun to apply a careful strategy of reminding him of his wife whenever he did, he was still a pain in the ass and he never missed an opportunity to ogle her.

What the hell do you want? "James," Tiff said dryly.

He put his hand into the pockets of his slacks, his creepy smile still in place.

Tiff suppressed the urge to shudder. "Can I help you with something?" she asked blandly. "Otherwise, I'm kind of busy."

He cleared his throat. "Actually, I was wondering if you were coming to the brunch on Saturday."

Tiff blinked. She'd forgotten the biannual brunch for the department was this weekend. "Not sure."

She did have friends in her department, and she wouldn't mind seeing some of them outside of a meeting or student review panel. But she wasn't about to let James think she was going to come based on his nudge.

"Well, think about it." James's grin widened. "It would be nice to see you there. We never get to hang out outside of work, you know?"

And that is completely by choice. Tiff fought for a smile but had a feeling it was a grimace that won. "I hope your wife will be able to make it so I can finally meet her."

James flinched, and Tiff fought hard not to roll her eyes.

Tiff leaned around him, calling through the open door to Liv Demora, one of the other history professors, as she walked by.

"Liv!" Tiff smiled at James for real this time as Liv veered into the room, abandoning whatever destination she'd had. "James was telling me he's bringing his wife to the weekend brunch. She's eager to meet more of his coworkers in the department. Will you be there?"

Liv grinned and exaggerated the movement when she nodded her head. "Oh most definitely. And meeting your wife will be a bonus, James."

Tiff's mood was improving by the second. "You know, maybe we can convince her to come to more things. I feel like we should get to know our colleagues' spouses, don't you?"

She leaned her chin on her crossed hands and looked at James with innocent eyes.

The pinched-mouth expression on his face told her she was describing his worst nightmare.

"Sure," he said, hurrying to leave the room, "I'll see if she can make it."

He wouldn't, but that was okay. He was walking away and that's all Tiff needed.

Liv didn't hide an amused laugh as she made her way to Tiff's desk and sat on the corner of it. "Nicely played."

"Are you going?" Tiff asked. "I'd honestly forgotten there

was a brunch this weekend."

"That's because you work too much," Liv said, pointing a finger at Tiff. "You've got tenure. I don't know if you got the memo, but you can ease up now."

Tiff didn't bother with a defense. They'd had this conversation before, but people had a hard time believing Tiff enjoyed her work to the extent she did.

Liv looked out the way James had just gone. "Not to mention, you can report his ass now that you have tenure."

Tiff waved a hand. "It doesn't matter. As soon as I mention his wife, he leaves. In fact, he hardly ever bothers me at this point."

It was only the fact she'd had a crap day that she had let him get to her at all today.

Liv moved on just as quickly as Tiff had. "I'll go to the brunch if you go. I hear the food is going to be good."

It was true. It was being held at a nearby restaurant famous for fluffy pancakes and a house-made berry syrup people raved about.

Tiff never could resist a good pancake. "Deal," she said, turning back to her work.

Liv waved her fingers over her shoulder as she left.

Tiff sipped her cooling tea and took a clearing breath, ready to dig into the new information she'd gathered from Shauna earlier in the day. There was one problem though.

Agitated all over again, she pushed around the papers, folders, and notebooks on her desk, running her fingers through the stacks.

"Dammit," she muttered, starting over at the first stack. It was no use. The one notebook she needed most wasn't there.

She'd left it at the police station after meeting the detectives.

CHAPTER 6

RONAN HUNCHED OVER HIS DESK IN THE BULLPEN AND RUBBED at his temples, attempting to block out the unrelenting squeak coming from the chair to the right of him. He had the bad luck to sit next to Mark Jepsen, the biggest asshole in their department and arguably on the force.

No one liked Jepsen, but that hadn't made the man stop to reflect on his personality or the way he engaged. He was one of those people who knew he was an asshole but didn't care and never would.

And at the moment, his chair let out squeak after squeak as he rocked it back over and over like a six-year-old.

Ronan had been fighting a headache that pain meds hadn't been able to touch. The squeak grated on his nerves, adding to an unproductive day that wasn't getting them any closer to a lead in their case.

The warrant had come through on Noah Barrett's house, allowing them to enter it shortly after finding the contractor, but they hadn't uncovered anything there. As the officers who'd done the preliminary sweep had said, nothing seemed out of place.

Nothing screamed that Barrett had been assaulted and removed from the home by force. Nothing hinted at a reason to hate Barrett enough to want him to suffer enormous amounts of pain before he died. Nothing clued them in to any information Barrett might have had that someone would torture him to obtain.

Before they could call it quits for the day, Ronan and Zach had to submit requests for subpoenas to obtain Noah Barrett's work files and emails.

By the time they finished that, they were both mentally exhausted and had decided they would hunt down Barrett's maybe-girlfriend in the morning when they were both fresh.

Ronan opened his desk drawer and pulled out the small can of oil he kept there, pulling out the thin tube that extended from the opening for application. Without words, he stood and went to Jepsen's chair, clamping one hand on the man's shoulder to still him while Ronan bent to apply the oil with his other hand.

"What the fuck, butt dick!" Jepsen barked.

Ronan smiled but didn't answer as he went back to his desk.

It didn't take long for Captain Calhoun to call out his office door. "Three dollars, Jepsen!"

"Butt dick should count as one swear," Jepsen muttered.

"That's two more!" Calhoun shouted.

Zach grinned at Ronan. They'd debated whether the captain had superhuman hearing or an uncanny ability to know exactly what someone's response would be to him. Either way, Jepsen was digging a hole and Ronan was happy to sit back and let it happen.

Particularly now that he'd fixed the squeak.

"You have plans tonight?" Zach asked as he and Ronan were preparing to leave the station.

"My couch," Ronan replied.

Zach shook his head. "Me and Shauna are going out to eat. Wanna tag along?"

Ronan rolled his eyes. "No. I don't want to tag along as the third wheel with you and your girlfriend."

If Tiff was there, maybe...

Ronan halted, wondering where the thought had come from. Tiff Carson had been pretty. Gorgeous, really, and he'd been able to tell right away that she was one of those unassuming beauties who didn't realize how stunning she was.

None of that changed the fact that they would have nothing in common. She was an academic. He was anything but that.

"Are you reconsidering?" Zach asked.

"Huh?" Ronan blinked.

Zach narrowed his eyes. "You okay?"

"Just tired." Ronan grabbed his jacket, hoping getting away from the florescent lights of the precinct would help with the headache. "I'll see you tomorrow."

"All right, partner. Get some rest."

As Ronan headed to his car, he debated the intelligence of stopping for a beer to try to help with the headache. Haven Tavern was only a few blocks away from the station. He could soothe his head with a cold beer in a frosted mug and be home in less than an hour. He wasn't really in the mood for people, though.

Before he could unlock his car door, his sister Paula phoned. Though he loved all three of his older sisters, he and Paula had always gotten along the best, probably because they were closest in age. She also happened to have two children who had him wrapped around their pinkies.

He leaned against his hood and swiped to open the video call.

Paula's face appeared on the screen with a grin. "Your niece flushed a Barbie doll down the toilet. She claimed she just wanted to give Barbie a Jacuzzi bath." Paula rolled her eyes.

Ronan cracked a grin, this time a genuine one that put both sides of his mouth to work. "That's awesome."

"Awesome?" Paula scoffed. "If I end up needing a plumber, I'm sending you the bill."

"Is that Uncle Roo?" Paula's face was suddenly replaced with her daughter's round face and wildly curly brown hair. Five-year-old Cindy was grinning widely with cookie crumbs all over her mouth. It shouldn't have been a pretty picture, but it somehow was.

"Hi, Uncle Roo!"

"Hey, Cindy. How are you?"

"I'm fine." She lowered her voice to a whisper. "But Mommy is mad at Barbie."

"I heard. Next time, just let Barbie take a bath in the sink, okay? She doesn't want to be in the toilet. That's icky."

Cindy giggled. "Okay."

"Where's your brother?"

"Right here!"

The face on the screen changed again, and Ronan's ten-year-old nephew, Raphael, appeared. His face was no longer as round as it had been when he was a kid but other than that, he and Cindy were a match.

"Hi, Uncle Ronan." Raphael had decided recently that the nickname of Uncle Roo was too childish for him to use anymore.

"Hey, buddy. And how are you doing?"

"Okay."

"How's school?"

"Boring." He twirled a pencil in his hand. "Catch any bad guys today?"

Ronan chuckled. His nephew thought he had the coolest uncle in the world and was always so fascinated with the work he did as a detective. "I'm working on it. In the meantime, I see a pencil in your hand and it's the end of a weeknight. My detective skills tell me you're doing homework. When you finish, you tell your mom I said to give you a big, heaping scoop of ice cream."

"What about me?" Cindy cried off-screen.

"You too, sweet pea," Ronan said.

"Yay!" Cindy cheered. "Hurry up and finish your homework, Raph!"

Ronan laughed as Paula returned. "Looks like you've got your hands full this evening."

"Don't I always. Anyway, what are you up to?" Paula squinted into the screen examining his surroundings. "You still at work?"

"Just leaving."

"Hopefully for a hot date? You know, you really should settle down and give these kids some cousins to play with."

"Soon as you can hook me up with Halle Berry, it's a deal."

"I'll have her people call your people." Paula winked. "I need to go check Raphael's homework. Love you!"

"Love you too."

Ronan's phone screen went blank. His mood had lifted but the headache was chiseling away at it. They needed to hit this case hard early the next day. He should grab a shower and sleep, not a beer.

He turned to open his car door, but movement caught his eye.

Across the lot, a figure emerged from a Chrysler 200. He

hadn't paid much attention to the car when he first saw it pull into the parking lot. But now that a feminine figure he recognized had hopped out and was hurrying toward the police station, his attention was thoroughly captured.

"Tiffany?" he uttered. Before he knew it, he'd repeated the word, this time shouting her name into the night.

She halted, her posture tense as she turned and looked around, searching for the source of his voice.

Ronan jogged toward her, waving his arms. "Over here."

Tiff spotted him and hugged her arms across her chest. "Oh! Detective Cafferty..."

"Just Ronan is fine. Or do I need to call you Professor Carson?" He stopped a few feet away from her, realizing that might have come out as flirtation. That hadn't been his intention, but his head and mouth didn't seem to be in sync at the moment. He cleared his throat. "What brings you back here so late?"

"Relax. I wasn't here to bother you guys. I got the hint. You're busy. I just left my notebook in your office earlier today and came back to get it."

"It's okay. We were done for the night, but I can walk you up to get it." Ronan stepped forward to hold the door open for Tiff, shoving his free hand in his pocket to resist putting it on her back to guide her.

He led the way back to the bullpen where a few of the night shift of detectives had arrived and were bullshitting with their daytime counterparts.

Sure enough, a black notebook had been left behind at the corner of Zach's desk. Ronan swiped it up and turned to find Tiff closer than he thought she was. She stumbled and caught herself, putting a hand to his pec as she did.

Ronan had the idiotic thought he was glad his time in the precinct's gym meant he didn't have to worry she might be feeling anything other than hard muscle. Then all thought fled as the heat of her hand on his chest hit him. God, how he wanted that touch to be skin on skin.

Tiff's eyes flew to his, something that looked like panic in them, as she pulled her hand back.

Lovely. She was mortified at the touch while he was fantasizing about it turning into more.

He put a hand to his head, rubbing at it again. He shouldn't be here. He should be home sleeping.

"You have a headache?" she asked.

Ronan realized he'd closed his eyes, but he opened them now to find her frowning up at him.

"It's okay. I'll get some sleep and it will go away." At least he hoped it would so he could be on his A game the next day. He hated the idea that the sick bastard who'd beaten and killed Noah Barrett was running loose in the city.

Tiff looked around as she dug in her purse for something. "Do you have hot water here somewhere?"

Ronan blinked. "Huh?"

A slight flush crossed her cheeks but she pulled a small plastic bag from her purse and waved it at him. "I get headaches a lot when I'm working so I carry these around with me everywhere."

Ronan eyed the baggy like it might contain the kind of medicine you didn't buy at the pharmacy. Inside the clear plastic were what looked like tea bags, but they weren't the store-bought kind. They were thin paper filled with dark leaves and folded over at the top.

She waved it again. "I promise. It might look funny, but if you have a teapot here, I'll make you a cup. It's my grandmother's headache tea. Trust me, the woman knows what she's doing with tea."

His headache flared a bit as if to tell him to try the tea.

"I'm not normally a tea drinker." Why had he said that like there was something wrong with drinking tea? "I can try it, though, I guess," he added quickly when he saw her face fall.

She brightened with a smile that made him feel like a superhero and he kicked himself for being so damned fascinated with this woman.

Tiff looked around again. "Is there..."

"Oh yeah," Ronan said, realizing she'd asked about hot water. This time, he did put a hand to her back and steered the way to the small coffee room. The coffee was hell to drink so most of them avoided it when they could, but even the department couldn't mess up hot water.

She seemed to know what she was doing as soon as she saw the industrial coffee maker. She grabbed a mug from the drying rack by the sink and popped one of her home-made tea bags in before using a little red tab on the corner of the machine to fill the cup with hot water.

"Huh."

She gave him a sideways look and a smile. "You didn't know you could get hot water out of the machine, did you?"

"Caught me," he said, grinning at her.

When she handed him the mug, he gestured to a table. Then again, maybe she hadn't meant to stay while he drank it. Maybe she was going to pass it off and leave.

"I can answer some of your questions about Herschel Kenworth if you want." He wanted to kick himself. He didn't know what the hell he was doing here with her. He should have thanked her for the tea and walked away, but instead he was offering an interview he'd told her earlier he didn't have time to do.

Tiff pressed her lips together, assessing him before she

spoke. "You seem tired. Let's see how that tea works and then maybe I'll ask you a few questions if you're up for it."

"Fair enough," he said, pulling a chair out at the round table that sat to one side of the room.

"So, umm, how did you get in touch with Shauna?" Ronan asked, breaking the silence to keep himself from staring at Tiff as he took his own seat.

God help him, he was looking at the soft glow of her skin, plagued with thoughts of touching it—running a hand down the side of her face.

She didn't seem to pick up on the fact he was ogling her.

"Shauna and I have been friends for a long time. We grew up down the street from one another and our families are both Irish so we hung out a lot as kids. How about you? Did you grow up around here?"

Ronan shook his head. "No. I'm a Colorado native. Grew up there with my three older sisters," he answered.

Tiff nodded as she laid a napkin next to his drink and then removed the tea bag from the cup, squeezing the excess liquid out before laying it on the napkin.

"It won't taste very good if it over brews," she said and then gestured for him to take a sip.

He blew on the edge of the cup before tasting the brown liquid. He'd always thought of tea as dirty water, not something one should actually drink. This didn't taste all that bad, though. It had a slight peppermint taste to it but there were other flavors in there as well.

Tiff seemed satisfied with his progress on the tea. "Three sisters, huh? Did they give you a hard time growing up? It had to be fun being the only boy and the youngest."

Ronan chuckled. "They used to chase me around and torment me, until I turned eleven."

"What happened when you turned eleven?"

Ronan flexed his arm, showing her his bicep and loving the way her eyes heated at the action. He was such a caveman.

"I grew muscles overnight. Probably all the tree climbing and hiking. I didn't let them chase me anymore." He grinned at her. "But really, they aren't bad sisters. We're pretty close. And the muscles came in handy when I needed to protect them as we got older."

"Is that why you became a cop? A protective streak from taking care of your sisters?"

Ronan shrugged. "It seemed like a good fit."

Some of his desire to protect and do right by people who had been hurt came from his sisters, but more of it came from the bullying he'd gone through as a kid. He didn't want to share that with her, though.

"How about you? You seem pretty normal. What made you want to spend all your time researching gruesome murders?"

She frowned. "You make it sound so sinister when you ask it like that."

"Sorry. Detective humor, I guess."

She lifted her shoulders and let them drop. "People don't like talking about the ugly parts of our past so they white-wash it and sugar coat it. I hate it. History is ugly sometimes, and that ugliness deserves to be acknowledged so we don't repeat the same horrible mistakes. I like learning what drove people to behave the way they did, how they got away with it, and what stopped the people around them from recognizing that there was a problem."

Ronan nodded his head slowly. "I solve the crimes. You figure out why they happened in the first place."

"If I can."

She pointed to his nearly empty mug. "Is it helping?"

Ronan realized with a jolt that his headache was much better. In fact, it was almost gone.

"Good," she said without waiting for an answer, a smug smile on her face. "Told you I have magic tea."

He raised his hands in defense. "I will never doubt the power of your tea again." He realized his tea was almost gone and he wouldn't have any excuse to keep her there any longer.

That was a good thing, right? He didn't want to be sitting here falling for this woman. She wasn't right for him.

No, he was the one who wasn't right for her. Not at all.

"You said you hiked a lot as a kid?" she asked before he could convince himself it was time to leave.

"Still do."

"I love hiking," Tiff said.

Ronan couldn't help the smirk that slipped onto his face. She was so pretty and feminine, he had a hard time imagining a woman like her was into hiking.

"Probably not the kind I do," he said, but then realized he sounded like a complete dick. She threw him off. You'd think he was one of those boys on a playground who didn't know that teasing the girl you liked was a piss-poor way to show your feelings. His mom and sisters had raised him better than that.

"Oh?" She raised a brow. "And how many fourteeners have you done?"

Well damn. Her use of the slang term for climbing a mountain that peaked over 14,000 feet meant she wasn't kidding. She was a serious hiker.

He'd underestimated her. "I'm up to eighty-five," he said, "though some of the ones in Colorado I've done twice, so there's still a big list of ones I need to get to."

There were ninety-six fourteeners in the United States, so he had plenty to get to still.

Her smile was too cocky. "Eighty-seven."

He put a hand to his heart. "My ego is seriously injured. I thought for sure I had you beat."

She pointed a finger at him. "You deserve it for dismissing my hiking prowess so easily."

He laughed at that and raised his hands in mock surrender. "You're completely right. I'll never underestimate your clearly superior talents again."

She took a slight bow in her seat, laughing as she did.

"Tell me about your most memorable hiking experience," Ronan said, reluctantly finishing the last of the tea.

"This might take a while," she said, but when he gave her a shrug, she started in on a story about a climb to the top of one of the smaller fourteeners in Colorado.

Ten minutes later, Ronan felt like no time had passed as he watched her, her cheeks pink with laughter as she finished the story about her older cousins betting her she couldn't make it up the mountain faster than they could.

The boys spent most of the early part of the hike trying to convince her to stop, but she gave up on them and went at her own pace, leaving them behind halfway up.

"They never made it to the top," she said. "I passed them on the way back down and they had to admit they were planning to go just a bit past wherever I stopped before turning around so they could claim they'd done it. They never thought I'd make it more than a quarter of the way."

"They probably didn't make a bet like that with you again," Ronan said, liking the way she'd one-upped them.

Tiff shook her head. "They absolutely didn't."

She glanced at the clock on the wall. "Oh! It's getting late and you said you were on your way out earlier. She stood and pushed in her chair. "I should let you get some rest," she said.

Ronan stood, too, taking his mug to the sink to wash before walking Tiff down to the parking lot.

"I'll walk you to your car," he said, noting with a frown she'd parked at the back corner where the lighting wasn't as good. "You should park closer, and under a light. Always under a light."

She looked around and then shrugged. "I try to park far away from the entrances so I can get a little more exercise throughout the day. I do a lot of sitting when I'm deep into a project like this."

As she spoke, she turned to him, caught between his body and the door of her car. He hadn't meant to stand so close to her, but he didn't back away.

He could see her interest in him when she looked up, meeting his eyes, as she tucked an errant strand of hair behind one ear.

Ronan stared at that ear, noticing the freckles around it and finding them positively adorable. An uncontrollable urge to lean over and kiss that ear hit him.

From there, his gaze trailed to her lips. What would she do if he followed his gut and leaned over to kiss her? His urge to find out was so strong, it practically hurt.

But he couldn't. He wouldn't. This was all wrong, no matter how easy it had been to talk to her.

"I guess I should be going," she said, gesturing over her shoulder.

Just like that, the moment was over. Ronan let out a breath, feeling ridiculous about how his emotions were running away with him over a woman he'd only known for a day.

He took a step back so she had room to open the door.

When she'd gotten in, she rolled down the window and smiled. "It really was nice talking to you tonight, Ronan. We can schedule that interview whenever you have time, okay? No rush."

"Let's make it tomorrow then. Stop by the station and we'll talk about your research. Go home and get your list of questions ready."

"Will do. What time should I come?"

Ronan thought for a moment. He suspected the morning would be filled with diving into Barrett's case again, going over whatever new information may have popped up overnight. But by afternoon, hopefully things would have slowed down a bit. Or at the very least, he would be able to take a break. "Afternoon should be fine."

"See you tomorrow afternoon then." With that, Tiff started her car and pulled away.

Ronan stood still until Tiff had driven off.

"You've lost your touch, man." He shook his head at himself as he walked to his own car.

Any other woman, he wouldn't have hesitated to lean in and kiss her. He would have known just where he stood with her and he wouldn't have questioned or doubted himself.

But with Tiffany Carson, he was like an awkward teenager all over again, so unsure of himself and what he was doing. And still listening to the voice in his head that said he was all wrong for her. That if she found out he could barely scrape out a passing grade when he was in school, she wouldn't look at him the way she had.

Sure, he might get a couple of weeks of mind-blowing sex before she figured out he wasn't worth more than that, but something told him with her, he'd want a lot more than that.

CHAPTER 7

RONAN KEPT HIS ATTENTION ON THE CONGESTED NEW HAVEN traffic as he navigated the department-issued navy-and-gray SUV he and Zach used as a second office toward Yasmine Bray's law firm, but he felt his partner's eyes on him from the passenger seat. Thankfully they didn't need to go through the center of town but traffic at seven thirty in the morning was heavy all over the city.

"Problem, partner?" he asked.

Zach's grin was slow, and he raised his hands for effect. "No problem here. Just wondering why you haven't told me yet that you had coffee with Tiff last night."

"Tea," Ronan said, then wished he could bite back the word.

Zach's amusement was plain as he put a hand to his stomach as though the laughter he let out was just too much to contain.

"Tea. I stand corrected. You had tea with Tiff and you didn't want to tell me about it?"

Ronan wanted to snap at Zach that there was nothing to tell. He wanted to demand to know what the hell was so funny about him having tea with Tiff. He didn't do any of those things.

He loosened his hands on the wheel on purpose and glanced at Zach. "Nothing to tell. I had a headache. She had tea that helped it. That's all."

"So she was nursing you back to health?"

Ronan didn't answer.

"She called Shauna and said you have a lot in common."

Ronan thought about that. They didn't really. They both loved hiking but that was about it. She spent her days surrounded by books and people with advanced degrees who probably debated quantum physics or some shit like that over breakfast.

He ran down criminals and turned them over to the lawyers and judges to deal with.

He loved what he did, and he was damned proud of it, but that didn't mean he and Tiff were on the same level.

"She's nice," he said, changing lanes when traffic opened up, and picking up speed. "And the tea worked."

Zach shifted fully in his seat to look at Ronan. This time Ronan looked his way but he couldn't read the look on his partner's face.

"You know, it's okay if you want to ask her out. Don't hold back or anything because she's friends with Shauna. I mean, provided you're not a dick to her."

"Good to know I have your blessing," Ronan dead-panned as he maneuvered onto a side street.

He made three more turns before pulling up in front of a small house that had been converted to an office. It boasted a lush green lawn and a stone sign that read: *Bray & Stein, LLP* with the words *Family Law* chiseled beneath the name.

Zach reached over and clapped a hand on Ronan's

shoulder. "Good, good. Glad we had this chance to talk," he said, his voice lowered like he was a father talking to his son.

Ronan laughed but shrugged off his partner's hand and opened the door.

Seconds later, they entered the house to find a wide entry with hardwood floors that looked original to the building, though they'd been stained and polished to a shine. A broad staircase of matching wood stood to the left of them and a living room to the right served as a waiting room and reception area.

The reception desk was empty but a round woman with light brown hair, pale skin, and pink cheeks came from the hallway beyond the stairs.

"Can I help you?" she said, an open smile on her face.

They held up their badges in unison. Ronan gave their standard introduction before asking if she was Yasmine Bray. She was in her late forties or early fifties, so it was possible she was Barrett's girlfriend.

Nothing overtly changed in the woman's expression, but there was a tension there. Chances were the legal community had heard of Barrett's death.

"No, I'm Kendall Stein, Yasmine's partner. I'll let Yasmine know you're here."

Yup. The woman knew about Barrett. If she didn't, she would have asked what they were there for.

Moments later, a slender woman with sandy brown hair tied back in a tight bun emerged from the back of the building. She wore a gray pencil skirt and a flowing white blouse.

If Ronan guessed right from the red eyes and pink nose, she'd been crying.

"I'm Yasmine Bray," she said. "You're here about Noah?"

Ronan nodded then gestured toward the back of the building. "Is it all right if we talk in your office?" he asked.

Ms. Bray blinked and then nodded. "Yes, sure. This way, please."

Ronan and Zach followed her up the staircase and into an office at the far right corner of the building. A brown leather love seat with a small glass oval coffee table filled one side of the space, with a matching brown leather chair behind a dark wood table being used as a desk.

There was a plant on one corner of the table and a red coffee mug with pencils and pens in it on the other. With the exception of a computer monitor and telephone, the rest of the desk was empty. Ronan wondered how she did that. He wasn't a slob, but he usually had a stack of files in one corner of his desk and a few sticky notes reminding him of tasks he needed to complete.

"Take a seat." Ms. Bray waved a hand to two smaller leather chairs in front of her desk.

When Ronan thought of family law, he thought of the attorneys who represented children taken from their home due to neglect or abuse. Often, those were lawyers working pro bono on behalf of the child.

He got the feeling this firm was doing much more than that from the look of things. Probably divorces and maybe drafting wills or something like that.

"Ms. Bray," Zach began, "you've heard Noah Barrett was found dead yesterday morning?"

Her eyes filled with tears again, but she seemed to keep them at bay through some sheer act of will. "Yes, Kendall and I heard half an hour ago."

"It's our understanding you were in a relationship with Mr. Barrett?" Ronan said, wanting to move the interview along. If she'd only just found out, he wanted to take advantage of the shock and see what she knew.

Ms. Bray shook her head. "No...I mean, well, we *were* in

a relationship. Were, as in past tense. We broke up." She took a tissue and dabbed at her eyes. "I'm not even sure I would call it a relationship, really. We just had a few dates here and there. It never turned into anything serious. Noah wasn't a serious relationship kind of man…"

Ronan made a note as Zach pushed for more.

"Can you elaborate on that?"

Ronan had his shit meter turned on, but he wasn't picking up anything. She seemed genuine.

They waited patiently, not adding to the silence.

Ms. Bray raised her brows. "Noah had a reputation among women in this field. We all knew that long-term dating wasn't his thing, not since his wife died. Some women didn't particularly like that about him, but it didn't bother me. I knew who he was when we started going out and hadn't been counting on it to turn into anything serious. There were no hard feelings from my end when it was over." She shrugged her shoulders. "Like him, I was looking for fun, and that's what I got."

Ronan took notes as he thought about what she'd said.

Up until now, he'd been harboring the image of a heart-broken middle-aged man who had never recovered from the death of his wife, and consequently spent all his time working. When they were told he might have a girlfriend, he'd added the possibility of a mending heart to his mental sketch.

Noah Barrett having a playboy reputation was new information, but was it something that might motivate a killer?

Ronan knew the answer to that was a big hell yes. An angry woman or the husband of someone Barrett shouldn't have been with. Both might be angry enough to want to inflict the kind of pain Barrett had endured.

"How did you meet Mr. Barrett?" Zach asked, continuing the interview and pulling Ronan out of his thoughts.

"I'd known Noah for years before we ever dated. We went to school together."

At her answer, Ronan glanced up at the framed diploma on the wall behind her. "New England Law School?"

She nodded. "Yes."

"And when was the last time you spoke to him, or saw him?" Zach asked.

She sighed. "I don't know. It's been a while. Maybe about a month or so ago?"

Ronan noted this and the fact it lined up with what they'd been told about her attending a company function with Barrett about a month ago.

"Okay. Even though you weren't in contact with him recently, is there anything you can think of that would have led someone to want to harm him?" Zach asked.

Ms. Bray shook her head slowly, a crease forming in her brow. "I don't know…"

"Do you know of any women he dated after you—or before you, even—who seemed particularly upset with him?" Ronan asked.

"Like I said, he had a reputation. But no one woman stands out in particular. No one that I think was upset enough to actually want him dead. I'm sure a lot of women probably wanted an explanation from him, so it doesn't help if he's dead, now does it?" She sighed. "And in all honestly, I knew about his serial dating, but didn't make a habit of keeping up with it."

"Okay. How about the cases he was working on?" Zach shifted gears. "Did he ever speak to you about any case that was giving him trouble? Any clients giving him a hard time? Or maybe a case linked to gambling or drugs?"

Bray gave them a look. "When we were together, we didn't discuss work-related things. We didn't discuss much of anything, to be honest."

"All right, thank you." Zack turned his gaze to Ronan, giving him a look that silently asked whether there was anything else he wanted to get out of Yasmine Bray.

Ronan shook his head. As someone who hadn't been in contact with Noah Barrett for at least a month, he doubted there was any more information she could give them. Besides, she had given them a new insight into Barrett's character, and that was helpful enough.

"Thank you for your time, Ms. Bray. We'll be in touch if there's anything else we need from you," Ronan said.

She stood and shook each of their hands. "Please, offer my condolences to the family. Noah may not have been an angel, but he didn't deserve to meet such a horrible end."

Three hours later, Ronan sat at his desk with a banker's box of files spread out in front of him. They'd gotten a warrant for Barrett's cases, and the firm had sent anything he was actively working on. Other than the Whitworth case, nothing jumped out as something that would be worth killing over.

Even with the Whitworth case, Ronan had a hard time seeing how someone would think harming Barrett would affect the case.

Unless there was some piece of information Barrett might have had that the killer wanted. Something that would explain the torture.

He didn't see anything to suggest Barrett or his firm were involved in anything shady or criminal.

Zach reentered the bullpen and tossed a file at Ronan. "Medical examiner's report."

"Excellent. What've we got?"

He skimmed through the report, noting that Noah Barrett had been killed somewhere between six and nine o'clock Sunday evening. Other than that, the report pretty much confirmed what they'd already known. Noah Barrett had been beaten to the point of suffering broken bones and killed before being thrown from the fourth floor.

"Nothing on the tox screen," he commented with a frown.

"You're thinking if it was a scorned woman, she'd have had to drug him to get him to the building?" Zach asked. Barrett was a large man. It would take a strong woman to take him out without some kind of help.

Ronan shrugged. "Possibly. Though if he was drugged, a woman or smaller man would need a way to transport him."

Zach nodded. "Maybe he was lured to the building somehow? Someone could have told him they needed legal advice before leasing it or maybe said they had something personal to discuss and wanted to meet out of the way so no one would see them together?"

Any of those things were possible, but they had nothing that pointed one way or the other. Before he could think much further on it, he heard the chime of an incoming email. He turned to his computer. "Got an email from the forensics department."

"Yep, I see it too," Zach said, looking at his own computer. "Nothing very helpful was found at the scene either. Damn, this case is a bust."

Ronan reluctantly had to agree with that statement. There had been a shoe print in the blood at the scene, but it was too smudged to garner any useful information from, like a shoe size.

Maybe in time, the identification division of the NHPD might match it to a sample on file and extrapolate a size from there. For now, all they could deduce was that *maybe* it came from a running shoe.

There were no fingerprints, hair samples, or anything else that could help identify the perp. The only DNA found was for the victim.

"How the hell did this perp manage to leave no evidence behind?" Ronan said, baffled.

Zach was frowning. "We're dealing with a skilled murderer here. Someone who was extremely careful and knew what they were doing. Someone who wore gloves, had their hair covered up."

"Someone who's done this before." Ronan turned to his computer, a bad feeling creeping up his spine. "We need to look at similar cases. If our perp is a professional, he...or she...must have done this kind of job in the past."

"Can you remember hearing about any cases similar to his?" Zach asked.

"Not in New Haven. But who's to say something like this hasn't happened out of state? We need to look in surrounding states, see if anything matches up."

Zach slid closer to his computer, and both he and Ronan fell silent as they set their sights on looking for a killer who'd practiced his craft before.

"Got it!" Ronan said twenty minutes later. "Springfield, Massachusetts." He grimaced as he relayed the details. "There was a seventy-two-year-old woman who was beaten in an abandoned garage. Cause of death was a slit throat."

Zach let out a whistle. "When was that?"

"Four years ago. Her name was Gretchen Meyer, and the

case is unsolved." Ronan met Zach's gaze. "And get this. Six months later, there was an eighty-year-old man killed even more brutally. Broken bones, burns, throat cut, and left in an empty building. His case is also unsolved. William Acavedo," he read off the screen.

"Still in Springfield, Massachusetts?"

"Yep, and then nothing after that."

Zach nodded. "Worth checking into then. I found some stuff too. But not as juicy as what you've got."

"Let me hear it."

Zach clicked around with his mouse, moving the screen toward Ronan. "A few unsolved cases in other parts of Massachusetts that involved beatings before the victims were killed and left in alleys. No slit throats though, so these cases don't entirely follow the pattern."

Ronan shrugged. "We're short on leads though, so the fact that they're in Massachusetts is reason enough to take a closer look at them."

"True. Let's put some of our junior detectives on these then. Have them look into the details more and see what they find."

"And we'll look into the Springfield murders," Ronan said.

He knew in his gut the murders would be linked somehow. They were hunting the worst kind of killer—a killer with confidence. There was nothing worse than someone who knew how to get away with murder.

CHAPTER 8

BY AFTERNOON, RONAN AND ZACH HAD PULLED OTHER detectives in on the case, to look at the similar unsolved murders in Massachusetts. By afternoon, they were putting together a murder board and filling it with all the information currently at their disposal. They were now a team looking at something much bigger than the homicide of one man.

Ronan studied the board, which, of course, he'd volunteered to set up.

On one side of the board, he'd written Noah Barrett's name in careful block letters, and everything they currently knew about him. On the other side of the board, he'd written the names of the two victims whose cases matched Barrett's most closely.

While no major breakthroughs had occurred yet, the process of writing things out on the board had helped Ronan organize his thoughts. Plus, it made him feel as though they were actually getting somewhere with this case.

"All right," Zach said, his hands on his hips as he read the board, "now things feel official. We're going to find this murderous, torturous bastard. My gut is telling me the same creep really is behind these cases. Has to be a local guy. And he doesn't travel more than a few hours at a time."

"It could be a woman. We can't cross out the possibility that a woman is behind this, given what Yasmine Bray told us," Ronan reminded.

They all knew the danger of making assumptions about the gender of a killer. They'd had a recent case with a sniper making some incredibly hard shots from distances most trained snipers couldn't make.

Profiling told them they were likely looking for a man based on statistics, but in the end, their killer had been a woman.

"Hell hath no fury like a woman scorned," Zach murmured.

"Such a sexist saying. Men are just as capable of violence when wronged," a female voice said behind them, and both men turned around in surprise.

Despite all his attempts to tamp down his reaction to her, Ronan's eyes lit up at the sight of Tiff Carson.

She was escorted by a uniformed officer, but Ronan didn't notice much other than her. She was dressed in a burgundy button-up blouse and black slacks, looking professional and effortlessly sexy at the same time. Her dark hair was pulled into a high ponytail, which called even more attention to her delicate neck and face.

Yes, he was looking at that neck and thinking of making her moan as he ran his tongue over it, nipping her with his teeth just behind the soft curve of her ear.

Yes, he was a pig.

No, he couldn't stop.

"Have a guest for you guys," the officer said.

Zach shot a glance at Ronan, and Ronan bit back a

curse. He'd forgotten he told her to stop by that afternoon. He was an idiot.

"Yeah, thanks," Ronan said, dismissing the uniformed officer.

"Tiffany. Hi..." Zach said. "I knew we'd be meeting again. I just didn't know it was today."

"You didn't?" Tiff looked at Ronan.

"I'm sorry," Ronan said, meaning it. "I forgot to mention it. Things have been so busy."

She cleared her throat. Though her expression was nonchalant, Ronan was pretty sure he detected disappointment.

The pig in him pumped a fist. If she was disappointed, that meant she'd been wanting to see him.

Unless she was only annoyed she wouldn't be able to ask him about the Kenworth case.

Damn. The pig deflated.

"Looks like I caught you guys at a bad time again," Tiff said. "I can just come back another time..."

"No. This is our fault. We forgot to work out a time that works best for us all, didn't we?" Zach said, looking at Ronan and sounding like an annoyed parent.

Tiff waved her hand dismissively. "It's all right."

"No, no..." Zach stepped forward. "We're not going to keep making you go back and forth." He nodded at Ronan. "We can kill two birds with one stone. I'll reach out to the Massachusetts detectives and report back to you. You take Tiff for coffee and answer whatever questions she has."

"Are you sure?" Tiff asked, looking uneasy.

"Positive." Zach winked and grinned as he walked away.

"You're sure this isn't an inconvenience?" Tiff glanced sideways at Ronan a few minutes later as they walked to a nearby coffee shop.

Knowing the coffee at the station tasted like industrial glue, Ronan insisted they go out, especially since a decent coffee shop was within walking distance.

He shook his head in response to Tiff's question. "No, not at all. I needed a break. Besides, it was my fault for losing track of time and not saying anything to Zach sooner."

"You mean your fault for forgetting about me?" Tiff teased.

"I could never forget about you. Trust me." He grinned at her and watched her cheeks turn a warm peach at his words.

He held the door for her at the shop and walked in after her, the rich aroma of coffee filling his nose. "Why don't you get us a table?" Ronan suggested as Tiff was about to head into the ordering line. "I'll get our drinks."

"Oh...thanks. A chai tea, please."

"Anything else? Bagel? Donut?" Why did he have an insane urge to feed this woman. What the hell was that about?

"Sure." She glanced at the glass case by the register. "A glazed donut please."

A few minutes later, Ronan found the table Tiff had selected—a small round one in the corner of the shop, away from prying ears. He set down her tea and glazed donut, and sat down across from her with his black coffee and chocolate donut.

"Thanks. It'll be my treat next time," Tiff said.

Ronan's heart skipped a beat, very much liking the sound of "next time." He took a sip of his coffee to keep himself from grinning too hard.

And reminded himself this was about her work.

And that she was way out of his league.

He'd already started formulating ways around that issue. Zach had said he didn't care if she and Ronan dated, so long as Ronan wasn't a dick to her. If he made it clear to her that this wouldn't be more than a few weeks of amazing sex, that would protect her feelings, right?

They could have fun and part amicably at the end of it.

It was a solid plan, so long as she was okay with that arrangement.

"So," Tiff pinched off a piece of her donut, "things are just as busy today, I see."

"Busier than ever. I had a feeling straight from the start this case wouldn't be easy. It's blowing up as we speak." He held up his coffee cup. "But I do need to recharge so it's not a bad thing you're making me take a break. There are days we don't eat or drink for most of a shift."

Tiff shook her head. "Not a good habit."

He tilted his head at her. "Why do I have the feeling you're guilty of getting sucked into your work for hours at a time?"

Her grin was immediate. "Guilty, but don't spread that around. I don't usually admit it. I guess the pressure of your badge got to me."

He grinned right back at her and pulled out the notebook he'd grabbed from his desk drawer before they left. It was the one that had his notes related to Herschel Kenworth. "I don't know if I can be much help in your research. We never did find out much about Herschel Kenworth. Hell, you might even know more than we do and can fill us in on some things."

As he spoke, Ronan opened the notebook and pulled out an erasable pen, though the latter was mostly out of habit. Once he was finished with a case, he wouldn't make changes to the notes so that the case was preserved as he'd written it at the time.

Tiff's brows creased as she put down her donut and leaned in to examine his notebook.

She pointed at his pen. "Do you always use an erasable pen?"

He didn't know where she was headed with this, but he nodded just the same. Her finger traced his writing in the notebook. Any other person and Ronan might have snatched it back, her actions reminding him too much of the bullying and taunting he'd received as a child.

He often only wrote part of a word down, but because he did that routinely, it wasn't a problem for him to understand what he'd written. And he always marked the margins of the small sheets of paper with a ruler before he started a new notebook to help with his spatial layout on the page.

He worked on that at home once every couple of months and then brought the stacks of notebooks to work so they were ready when he needed one.

She looked up at him, her face scrunched as she clearly worked on something. She pointed to where he'd crossed something out by making a neat box around it and drawing an x that went from all four corners and extended through the center.

"Why cross out if you use an erasable pen?"

Ronan hesitated. He wasn't used to explaining his notation style to anyone other than the kids he worked with at the tutoring center, but he didn't see any cruelty or taunting in her gaze. Only genuine puzzlement.

He cleared his throat. "If I make a mistake on a single word or letter, I'll erase it. If it's something larger than that, it gets too messy to erase. I use the box for that."

She tilted her head, looking back down at his notes

before looking back to him. "This might sound completely out of left field if I'm wrong, but were you diagnosed with dysgraphia as a child?"

Ronan stiffened, his guard up. He didn't get a lot of people commenting on his handwriting anymore. When he first came to the major crimes division, Jepsen tried to make a big deal out of how carefully Ronan wrote, using block letters that he knew he'd be able to read later.

Ronan despised bullies, and he wasn't a kid anymore, so he shut that shit down with Jepsen fast and hard, making sure the other detective knew he wouldn't put up with that shit.

Tiff must have seen his tension, because she rushed to explain, reaching her hand toward him across the table. "I'm sorry. That's a really personal question, I guess. And probably a weird one. I only asked because my little brother has dysgraphia."

Her words came quickly and her cheeks had that peach tinge they got when she was embarrassed. Despite his initial reaction to her question, Ronan's mouth quirked at the way she got all cute when she was flustered. She was a woman with a doctorate in history who stood up in front of a room of people to lecture, but here she was looking frazzled as she tried to explain where she was going with the topic.

"He's younger than me. A lot younger. He just turned ten. My parents had me really young and then him really late so there are a lot of years between us. Anyway, he was diagnosed with dysgraphia when he was six and I recognize some of what you do from the occupational therapist who works with him on his writing and spatial issues."

She shook her head. "And if you don't know what dysgraphia is, then you have no idea what I'm talking about and this is just confusing and maybe a little offensive to you."

Ronan couldn't stand it anymore. She was cute, but she was starting to squirm like she was really uneasy and unsure and he didn't want to make her feel that way.

"I was," he said. "Not until I was much older than six, though. My teachers thought I was lazy and stupid until my mom figured out what was going on when I was twelve and educated them on the topic."

Lazy. Stupid. Dumb. Those words had all come out of teachers' mouths, and even when they weren't saying it right to his face, he always heard it. Always.

When he was a kid, a lot of teachers didn't understand dysgraphia. If they'd known how much work Ronan and his mom had to do to overcome the issues his dysgraphia caused, they would never use the word lazy to describe him. His mom had researched the disability and found everything she could on ways to manage it.

She made sure his teachers let him have extra time on tests after that and didn't mark him off for poor handwriting, but she also came up with all kinds of exercises they did at home on top of his normal homework assignments. The things she did with him showed him he wasn't stupid. That there wasn't something wrong with him.

Tiff pointed to the margin on one side of the page. "Mick's therapist printed out a template he uses in class with heavy margin lines and wider ruling to help him. It's interesting to see that this helps you."

Ronan felt himself relax as he realized she was eager to talk to someone with the same learning disability her brother had. "Yeah, it definitely helps. I tutor kids at a nonprofit on the east side and several of them have dysgraphia. Others have things like dyslexia and ADHD. I bring old notebooks with key information redacted to show them that even though there isn't a cure for their learning disability, they can learn ways to overcome the symptoms of their diagnoses."

She was practically beaming at him and he couldn't believe he'd once thought she might be like his teachers. That she might look down on him for something like this. He liked the way she was looking at him now. A lot.

Why had he thought she would be like the teachers he had as a kid just because she was in academia? Clearly, she was nothing like them. And it was plain she didn't look down on her brother for his differences. Maybe she wouldn't look down on Ronan for them, either.

Tiff seemed to shake herself and looked at her watch. "Sorry. We haven't even touched on the Kenworth case and I've already taken up a lot of your time."

Ronan took a slow sip of his coffee, not taking his eyes from her, before answering. "I still have time."

It wasn't entirely true, but the break was doing him good. Being with this woman was doing him good. He knew when he did go back to the case, he'd be better for it. He'd be fresh and might see something they hadn't before.

She took her own notebook from her bag, this one a full-sized red spiral lined pad instead of the small pocket ones he used. She started with one of the tactics they used in interrogations, opening with a broad question instead of something specific. "What can you tell me about the Kenworth murders?"

"When we first caught the Liz Gordon case, our medical examiner saw the similarity to the old Marsh Killer cases. Once we realized we weren't dealing with a copycat killer, but rather, someone who had the actual lipstick and rope from the old crimes, we ended up digging into those past murders."

This was all information he could discuss with her. The lipstick and rope evidence had all come out in the trial of Liz Gordon, along with the fact that the cut ends of the rope used on the last murder victim from thirty years prior matched the cut ends of the rope used on Liz Gordon's first victim.

"At that point, were you trying to figure out who could possibly possess the same murder weapons your cold case killer had been using? Or were you wondering if the cold case killer was back?"

"We hadn't narrowed it to one or the other and there wasn't much from the cold case to lead us to the killer. We began to focus on any possible explanation for the murderer to stop and then start again after such a long period of time." He knew he didn't need to explain to her that a serial killer wouldn't simply stop. She would know that from the work she did.

She nodded. "Travel, prison time..."

"Exactly." He couldn't tell her that they'd focused on the grandfather of one of Liz Gordon's neighbors because he traveled for business. They had thought he might be using a different killing ground to satiate his urges. That came too close to one of the issues Liz Gordon's attorneys might raise in her appeal.

Tiff smiled and clutched her coffee mug as if to warm her hands. "And then you focused on mental institutions."

He nodded. "We didn't see the link immediately because Kenworth was Liz Gordon's mother's maiden name." He was getting too close to the details of how they zeroed in on Liz Gordon, so he shifted gears. "We never found any journal or letters that explained Kenworth's motives, but by all accounts he struggled with mental illness throughout his life. And I don't think he received the best of care. He seemed to be the family's dirty little secret."

Tiff leaned toward Ronan, her eyes intent on him as her expression grew dark. "I've read the reports of his lobotomy and it's stunning for that time period. It must have been one of the last lobotomies to be done in the United States."

Ronan agreed. "The family was wealthy and powerful and they discovered Herschel was behind the murders. Rather than deal with the scandal of having a serial killer in the family, it seems they went to his treating psychologist and convinced him to commit Herschel and perform the lobotomy. I have to wonder if the doctor who performed it knew why they wanted it."

Tiff nodded. "It's hard to believe that in the late seventies he genuinely believed a lobotomy was the best course of treatment for his patient, but I'll need more than conjecture before I go there. It could be that the family paid him or it could be they told him they'd discovered he was the Marsh Killer and the doctor felt this was a way to protect the community from a killer."

Ronan pushed his empty coffee cup away and rested his forearms on the table. "I'm sure you know the doctor is dead, but I wonder if you can track down any of his children."

He thought about Liz Gordon's confession. He didn't want to delve into the details of that, but she had told them she overheard her grandfather talking to her father on his deathbed. The grandfather found the lipstick and rope and knew Herschel was the Marsh Killer. They'd immediately had him committed to the mental institution and the lobotomy was performed shortly after that.

"Maybe the doctor left behind a journal or spoke to the

family about it before he died," Ronan said. "If he did perform the operation for anything other than medical reasons, it might have weighed on him."

Tiff made a note on her notepad before smiling at Ronan. "That's a great idea."

"And have you talked to Julia Sawyer? She lived next to Herschel and knew him when they were teens. They sometimes spoke in the back garden together. She was small and petite just like his victims were."

"I already tried talking to Julia Sawyer. I found out the Sawyer family put the house up for sale and moved out of town after their son was convicted of rape."

Tiff sighed. "I'll go see Liz Gordon in prison. Her parents left the country and aren't expected back anytime soon. They have a caretaker on the property that I tried to speak with, but he wouldn't talk. I spoke to a few people who went to school with Herschel before his parents had him institutionalized, but they didn't have much insight. I think Julia Sawyer might have been one of the only young people he engaged with much."

Ronan nodded. "I know it isn't easy, especially when gathering information is such a tedious process. Trust me, I know all about tedious information-gathering."

She grinned. "But it's what we do. Gluttons for punishment."

He laughed at that. "True. Just keep digging. Eventually, bits and threads will start coming together so that you can form a better picture."

Tiff smiled. "Thanks, Ronan. Once I figure out more of his story, I'll be looking at ways the crimes affected women and girls in the community during that time period and going forward."

"More than just the victims and their families?"

"Absolutely," she said with a nod. "Crime against women has a much broader impact than people realize. It's not just the victims and families. It's the entire community. Women make different decisions than men do based on the very fact they're women. They know being a woman might make them a target of violent crime."

Ronan nodded. In his line of work, he knew that all too well. He'd seen far too many women brutalized and knew it could destroy lives.

Tiff went on. "Violence against women is so entrenched in our history as a people that it affects every layer of life for women. The effects can be seen in our careers, in religion, in biases about who we should be or what we should do."

Ronan was fascinated listening to her and the passion she had for her work. He knew plenty of people were interested in true crime stories. It was the reason crime shows and documentaries were so popular. People in general had a morbid fascination with murder.

But Tiff was different. She wasn't just after the gory details for the shock factor of it all; she was interested in how and why these crimes happened, but she planned to use the information to teach a point that went far beyond the macabre details. What she was doing went so much deeper than the murders themselves.

CHAPTER 9

RONAN WHISTLED AS HE REENTERED THE BULLPEN. HIS COFFEE with Tiff had energized him. Hell, it had done more than that. He'd been an idiot to make assumptions about her without getting to know her. In that way, he'd been no better than the bullies he'd hated in school.

And even though his mind kept going back to her smile or the intense passion she had for her work, he was also energized to get back to his own case. To stopping whomever had killed Noah Barrett and likely several people in Massachusetts before this.

Zach looked up as Ronan approached their desks. "How did things go?"

Determined not to grin like a lovestruck schoolboy, Ronan forced his expression to remain nonchalant. "It went well. We talked about Herschel's case—or what we could regarding it, at least. She's still got some interviews to do. I probably wasn't as much help to her as she had been hoping, but..." Ronan shrugged his shoulders.

"All right. Well, we've got some news for you on this end.

Sort of." Zach sighed and folded his arms across his chest, while two other detectives in the unit, Cal Rylan and Jarrod Harmon, gathered.

"We were able to get in touch with the detectives from Massachusetts," Cal explained, "and after hearing what we're dealing with, they're convinced the murders are connected, too. They're sending everything their forensic teams found so we can try to confirm the link, though it's not much more than we have."

"It's something," Ronan said, glad they finally had a lead on the frustrating case. If the Massachusetts cases were truly connected, their killer wasn't going to stop on his own. They were racing against a clock and they didn't have any idea how much time they had before their killer struck again.

"Maybe." Jarrod frowned. "The victims don't seem to have anything in common, though. William Acavedo was a former prosecutor. Of course, the Massachusetts detectives looked at the cases he'd worked, but it's worth noting that he'd been retired almost twenty years before he was murdered. In his younger days, he'd prosecuted several homicides, but nothing really stood out. And as for Gretchen Meyer, she was a retired secretary. Worked for a physician before she retired so no link to the law like Acavedo and Barrett."

"Nothing noteworthy in the forensics?" Ronan asked.

Zach answered. "Nope. No hair, DNA, or fingerprints at either crime scene."

"Both victims were missing for several days before they were found though," Cal chimed in. "Just like our case."

Zach nodded. "Yeah, there's that. But still, neither case had any witnesses. According to the Massachusetts detectives, they thought they might be dealing with a serial killer, but then the crimes just stopped, so they weren't sure what to think. Never had anything to go on after that. They still revisit the cases each year, but..." Zach shrugged.

Ronan crossed his arms and frowned at the floor as he thought about what they knew. "Let's expand our search to other states. Maybe this killer traveled farther than just Connecticut and Massachusetts. Maybe we're dealing with someone who offs one or two people and then moves on. We've got to establish a pattern if we want any hope of solving this thing."

Ronan paused, a thought occurring to him.

"What is it?" Zach asked, narrowing his eyes.

"Hold on. Give me a second." Ronan retrieved his notes and flipped through the pages, taking a look at what he had jotted down during their interview with Yasmine Bray. "Yasmine Bray and Noah Barrett both went to New England Law School, remember?"

"Yeah. And?"

"That school is in Massachusetts."

Zach's eyes widened. "Oh shit. You're right. How did we overlook that?"

"We should find out when Yasmine moved here," Ronan said, his head thoroughly back in the game.

"Detectives." A uniformed officer approached, handing Ronan a slip of paper. "Captain said to let you know Noah Barrett's children are in town. They're staying at a hotel until his house is cleared for them to enter."

Ronan looked down at the paper to see the name of a hotel and room number. He didn't know if the children would have anything for them, but they would absolutely go see them. If for no other reason than giving them the courtesy of an introduction and an assurance that they were working as hard as they could to bring their father's killer to justice.

And then he wanted to dig into Yasmine Bray's history and find out if there was more to the family law attorney than they'd thought.

CHAPTER 10

Tiff opened the sheer white curtains of her office as wide as she could and refilled her mug with hot water from the kettle and a fresh bag of lavender tea. She added several drops of lilac essential oil to the electric diffuser she kept on her desk and pushed the power switch to start it working.

Her task that morning was one of the things she found hardest about her job, and she would need the scent and view of the sun to help her mood.

As the diffuser produced a pale tendril of spring-scented smoke, she spread out a twenty-four-by-eighteen-inch sheet of paper on her desk, smoothing her hand over it as she pulled out a pencil to make notes. Across the page, she'd written the names of each of Herschel Kenworth's victims, circling them. If he had left any surviving victims, she would have noted them here, but none of Kenworth's victims had escaped.

She'd made lines from each of the victims with circles at the end, inside of which she'd written the names of any surviving family members of that victim. Another circle contained notes about any deceased members of the victim's family.

Next she had contact information and notes about the person that were available online. It wasn't the kind of information that told the full story of who they had become but it was something, and even what was there was striking.

One parent had begun an organization that trained women and teens in self-defense in cities around the tristate area. Two people in her chart had died by suicide. One sister had become a police officer. Two brothers were in prison. Another sister had been arrested twice for driving while under the influence of a mind-altering substance.

An aunt had changed jobs, leaving her work as a nurse to serve as a minister in a church in the community where her niece had been killed. Others had moved away from the area, some going clear across the country.

It was time for Tiff to reach out to each of them to see if they wanted to share their stories in the hopes that what she was doing might help show people the far-reaching impact of violence against women. She wanted to do this in a way that would cause them the least amount of pain, but she also knew that when she raised the issue of their loss, it would immediately trigger the worst heartache they'd likely endured.

She had found over the course of doing this for several projects that sending a hand-written note to introduce herself instead of attempting to call or email worked best.

She pulled out a stack of plain sky-blue stationary and began to write. In each letter, she introduced herself and the project she was working on, explaining her goals for the project and her respect for their privacy.

She stressed that she would not harass them in any way, should they decide they didn't want to participate, and encouraged them to take all the time they needed to come to a decision. She provided her email and phone contacts and closed with her sincere regrets that their life had been touched in this way.

It would take her several hours to write to all of them but she always made the effort to ensure they knew she wasn't going to harass them like they'd been hounded by the media thirty years ago. She wanted them to know she saw them each as more than the family member of a victim of crime and would respect them and their wishes in her efforts to complete her work.

She knew she'd only hear back from a third of them at best, but she wanted to include their voices if she could.

"Our sincerest condolences to you all for your loss," Ronan said, taking in the three Barrett children and their varying levels of grief.

They were staying in a suite in one of New Haven's more expensive hotels and from the look of the jewelry and clothing they sported, they'd either invested Dad's money well or were pulling in impressive money of their own.

The two sisters perched on the edge of the hotel room sofa while the son took an oversized armchair next to the couch. Where the sisters had clearly been crying for some time, the brother had his legs spread wide in front of him, with an empty glass that held melting ice cubes and the remnants of what smelled like vodka in one hand. His eyes were dry.

The oldest of the children spoke first, her voice nasally and her eyes bloodshot as she clutched a used tissue. "Have you found anything out yet?"

"We have several leads we're looking into," Ronan said, glad that it wasn't a complete lie at this point. "But we do want to see if you have any information that might point us toward one lead over another in our investigation. Can any of you think of someone who might have had a problem with your father?"

The three of them exchanged glances, silently questioning each other. Not something Ronan wanted them doing. He wanted their gut reactions and thoughts, not a censored agreed-upon statement.

Zach pressed them. "Don't worry about whether something is important enough to mention or whether you're right or wrong about any hunch you might have. We want as much information as we can get now. We have other detectives working the case, running down everything we come up with, so the more you can tell us, the better."

"I never knew anyone to have any issues with Dad," the oldest daughter said. "Did either of you?"

The son, Barrett's middle child, shook his head. He bore a striking resemblance to his father in both his face and his build. "No. But Dad wasn't much of a talker. Do you think he would have told us if he was in some kind of trouble?"

"Probably not," the youngest admitted. She sniffed and wiped her nose, her head bowed. "I just can't believe this. Does Grandpa know yet?"

"Shit." The oldest buried her head in her hands.

The brother stood and went to the couch, lowering his large frame to sit between his sisters, and Ronan saw his veneer begin to break as he pulled his sisters against him.

Ronan would like to give them all the privacy and time they needed to process their loss, but they needed to garner any information they could sooner rather than later. The longer this killer went free, the less likely they would be to catch them. To stop them.

The grandfather was one more person who might be able to shed light on things. Detective work was a game of interviews upon interviews, building a story one small word or letter at a time. "Your grandfather? Is that your father's father or your mother's?"

The brother rubbed at his sisters' backs. "Dad's. He lives one town over. Eighty-one years old so news like this might kill him."

Zach exchanged glances with Ronan. "We were made aware of you three, but not your grandfather. No one on our end has contacted him."

"Don't," the oldest daughter said quickly. "We'll tell him now that we're here. He's not in the greatest shape as it is. And like my brother said, this is going to hit him hard."

"All right," Ronan said, "but we will want to speak with him as soon as you do."

If Barrett knew someone was out to get him, would he have been more likely to mention something to his father, who was local, or his kids, who were out of town?

Ronan didn't know, but they needed to find out soon.

CHAPTER 11

"ANYTHING MORE ON YASMINE BRAY?" ZACH ASKED, AS HE slid into the passenger seat of their SUV balancing two coffees.

Ronan looked up from his laptop, taking the coffee before answering. "She moved to Connecticut five years after law school and has been here ever since."

"So she wasn't in Massachusetts at the time of the other murders," Zach said, removing the top of his cup to blow on the liquid.

Ronan took his coffee with enough milk or cream to cool it and he was glad now as he took a large swallow.

"Massachusetts isn't a far drive," Zach said. "If she had some beef with the Massachusetts vics, maybe she had a reason to take a few days' vacation in her old state."

Ronan thought about what Zach said. He wasn't wrong, but it wasn't much. It wouldn't be enough to get a warrant or even bring her in for questioning, really.

Zach put the top back on his coffee and put it back in the cupholder between them before pulling out his phone and scrolling to pull up an email. "I got the background checks back on the lawyers at Barrett's firm. Finn Leland has an allegation of spousal abuse against him from his first marriage, but that was twenty-five years ago. He's remarried now and has been with his current wife for sixteen years. No allegations from her and no emergency room visits that scream of abuse that I could find. But I've added this to our follow-up list."

Zach shifted in his seat in the small confines of the car. "The associate, Marcus Jones, has no criminal record, but he does have family in Massachusetts. His parents and two brothers live there so there could just as easily be a link between him and the other victims as there could be for Yasmine Bray."

Ronan thought back to their interview with Marcus Jones. He hadn't detected anything particularly sinister about the man. But looks could be deceiving.

"Okay," Ronan said, "let's see if Leland, Jones, and Bray have alibis for Sunday evening, when Noah Barrett was killed."

Zach answered by way of dialing Finn Leland. He then placed the phone on speaker and set it down on the dash between himself and Ronan.

When they'd gotten through the secretary to Leland, Zach reminded him that they'd spoke to him about Noah Barrett.

"Yes, I remember," Leland replied, the tone of his voice growing somewhat guarded like he hadn't expected to hear from them again. "What can I do for you?"

Ronan listened, his notepad at the ready as Zach spoke.

Zach launched into the spiel they used for getting someone's alibi when they didn't want to alert the person they were looking at them as a suspect. Ronan wasn't honestly sure it would work with Finn Leland with his experience as a criminal attorney.

Zach tried to put that fact to work for them. "I'm sure I don't have to tell you that we need to rule out as many people as we can to build a solid case that will hold up to scrutiny down the road. We're looking at someone for Barrett's murder, but we need to eliminate anyone else involved in the case, no matter how tangentially. Can you tell me where you were this past Sunday evening, between six and nine o'clock?"

There was a slight pause before Leland answered, and when he did, there was the expected edge to the man's voice. No matter how much you soft-pedaled it, no one liked being on the receiving end of the alibi question.

"I work early hours, detective. Sunday evenings, I'm home with my wife getting ready for the workweek. This Sunday was no exception."

"Is there anyone else other than your wife who can confirm this?"

"My neighbors, surely. They would have seen my car in the driveway."

"And you didn't run any errands or step out between those hours? To a grocery store to pick something up for dinner. Or...I don't know, for a walk, or anything? At any point, did you leave your house?"

"No, I did not. I'd already gone grocery shopping Saturday afternoon."

Zach exchanged glances with Ronan, who simply shrugged.

"All right, Mr. Leland. Thank you. Enjoy the rest of your day."

"Likewise. Goodbye."

If they needed to, they would run his alibi down with the wife and neighbors.

"Now, let's see what Marcus Jones has to say." Zach dialed the number they had on file, and they went through much the same routine.

"I don't see that I need to answer that for you unless you have some reason other than dotting your Is and crossing your Ts."

Ronan held out his hand when Zach opened his mouth to answer and the two waited in silence.

Marcus did what Ronan knew he would. He filled the silence.

"I was at home." He waited a beat and then, "but I live alone so I'm not sure how that helps you."

Zach ran through the questions about errands and neighbors but Marcus couldn't come up with anyone who might have seen him.

It meant they couldn't cross him off their list, but they were in the same situation as they were with Yasmine Bray. There wasn't a whole lot to point toward him either.

"Is there anything else I can answer for you though?" Marcus offered, a hint of desperation entering his voice. He obviously understood that not having a solid alibi didn't do him any favors. "You know I'm willing to help in any way I can. I'm more grateful for Noah than I ever had the chance to tell him. He took me under his wing, you know? I got to do advanced work that other associates would kill to do, so if I can do anything to find out who did this, let me know."

Ronan frowned. If Barrett took this associate under his wing, had he gotten to the point where he'd benefit from Barrett's death by taking over on his cases? Or was Jones genuine in his offer to help?

Ronan leaned forward, letting Zach know he had a question to ask. Catching on, Zach slid the phone closer to him.

"Mr. Jones. This is Detective Cafferty. Is there anyone at the firm you have a strained relationship with? Any other associates who perhaps harbored jealousy over the fact that Noah Barrett had taken you under his wing?"

"Oh, I hadn't thought of it that way. I know some of the other associates wished they were in my position, but there wasn't outright animosity."

Jones sounded horrified at the thought and Ronan knew to most people it would be horrifying. But he'd seen people kill for less.

"All right. Thank you, Mr. Jones."

"Absolutely. Take care, detective."

After ending the call, Zach leaned back in his seat and sighed, staring out the windshield. "Marcus Jones doesn't have a good alibi, but he also doesn't have a great motive."

And Ronan had to admit, it wouldn't make sense for another associate to be their killer if the homicide cases in Massachusetts proved to be linked.

Zach picked up his phone. "Yasmine Bray next?"

Ronan frowned. "Let's hold off and see what else we can find out about her. See if we can find a connection to the Massachusetts deaths first."

He didn't know why but he thought there might be more to her than they were seeing and he didn't want to tip her off that they were looking at her if he could help it.

Zach agreed, setting to work sending messages on his phone. "Sounds like a plan. I'll have the others start to look deeper into her background and time in Massachusetts, see if anything pops."

While he was busy, Ronan pulled out his own phone and sent a message to Tiff. He wouldn't normally take any time off when they were on a case like this, but she'd invaded his thoughts from the start on this case.

Any chance you could meet for dinner tonight? I can't get away for long, but there's an incredible Thai place near the precinct. Let me buy you curry?

He grinned. It was cheesy but he thought she'd like it.

A moment later, as his partner smirked knowingly at him from the seat next to him, Ronan read her reply.

Love to! I'll come to the precinct at 7 and drag you out for a break.

Damn, it was like she knew him already.

CHAPTER 12

RONAN AND ZACH HAD JUST STEPPED FOOT INSIDE THE bullpen when one of the other detectives waved her arm over her head at them as she spoke into the phone at Ronan's desk.

They hustled her way and she covered the receiver. "Nicole Barrett says her grandfather has gone missing."

Ronan recognized the name of Noah Barrett's oldest daughter and took the offered receiver with a nod of thanks to the other detective.

"Nicole, it's Detective Cafferty. What's going on?"

She sniffed, obviously crying. "Grandpa didn't take the news of Dad's death well. An officer called us and said you'd cleared us to go to Dad's house so we brought him there so he wouldn't be alone."

Ronan glanced at the clock. It had only been a few hours since he'd seen Barrett's children so they couldn't have been at Barrett's house long. "Okay, and you told the detective he's gone missing?"

"He was sleeping," Nicole Barrett explained. "My brother and sister went to the funeral home to discuss

arrangements for Dad's funeral, and I went grocery shopping because there's no food in the house. When I got back
though, Grandpa was nowhere to be found."

"Are you in the house, Nicole?" She should have gotten
herself out of the house before calling him in case there was
someone in the house, but he doubted she had.

"Yes, but I looked all over for my grandfather and called
out to him. The house and the backyard are empty."

Ronan remembered the garage. "Did you check the
garage?" If she said no, he'd send an officer there to do it.
Zach was already on the phone with dispatch having a
patrol unit sent to the Barrett house.

"I did," she said. "He wasn't there."

This woman didn't have an ounce of self-preservation in
her body. Then again, she probably couldn't truly understand what this killer was capable of. She hadn't seen what
he'd done to her father, and though they'd told them their
father had been beaten, she was probably in denial to a
certain degree about what had happened.

"Okay." Ronan made his voice as soothing as possible.
"Does your grandfather have memory issues? Do you think
he got confused about where he was and wandered off?"

"No. His body is frail, but his mind isn't. He wouldn't
have done that."

"Okay, and how about any signs of forced entry. Any
broken glass or evidence of a struggle?"

"No break-in or anything but one of the couch pillows
was on the floor with a novel next to it like it had fallen."

"All right, Nicole. I want you to stay at the house in case
your grandfather comes back. Alert your brother and sister
about what's going on. I'm going to activate a Silver Alert for
your grandfather and send patrol officers to check the
neighborhood and surrounding areas."

"O-Okay," she stammered. "Thank you."

"No problem. I'll be in touch as soon as we find anything."

Ronan ended the call and immediately set to work. Zach had sent a patrol car and was in the process of activating Silver Alert for missing seniors.

Ronan knew Luis Barrett had likely just gotten confused, forgot he was at his deceased son's house, and wandered off to return to the home he lived in on his own.

On the other hand, if Luis Barrett had been abducted, it had to be their killer. What were the odds that the killer would go after the son, and then the father? Did someone have a vendetta against the Barrett family?

"Detective Cafferty, the contractor who worked on Noah Barrett's house is waiting to see you," an officer said, approaching Ronan and Zach's desks and gesturing to where he'd left the contractor, Ted Hadley, standing at the entrance to the room.

Ronan waved him in and watched as the man crossed the space, crossing by the uniformed officer who was leaving.

Hadley gripped his baseball cap in one hand and extended his other hand to Ronan.

Ronan shook, hoping the man wasn't here for nothing. As much as he believed Luis Barrett had simply wandered off, he wanted to get out there and look for him.

Still, Ronan made himself slow down and address the man in front of him. "Good to see you again, Mr. Hadley. Do you have something for me?" He gestured to the seat to one side of his desk.

Ted Hadley took a seat and rested his hat on his knee. "It's just, I can't get Noah Barrett out of my head. I keep trying to think of something that might be helpful, and late last night, something occurred to me."

"All right. Let's have it."

Ronan glanced at Zach who was off the phone and listening to Mr. Hadley as well.

"I've been thinking back to the times I came to work on the shelves over the weekend. In hindsight, I remember on that first day, there was a car parked across the street. Of course, I didn't think nothing of it at the time. But now, I'm not so sure. Maybe someone was watching the house, you know? Waiting for Noah or something."

"Do you remember what kind of car it was?" Ronan slid a pad and pen over and poised to write down any information.

"I think it was a black BMW. Not sure of the year or license plate or anything like that though, but I got a picture of it." He pulled a cell phone from his pocket and began scrolling through apps.

Ronan sat forward, hoping this was a break in the case. He saw Zach watching intently now as well.

Hadley spoke as he worked. "I was taking pictures of the side of Mr. Barrett's house. There was a section of the brick where the mortar in the joints was beginning to crumble. I was going to tell him about it and see if he wanted me to fix it while I was out there working on the shelves."

He looked up as though he'd found the picture. "I sent it to him, but he never replied."

Ronan wanted to snatch the phone from the man since he didn't seem like he was going to show them the picture anytime soon. He'd said he didn't get the license plate but sometimes people had a parking pass sticker in a window or a hangtag on a visor that let them enter a lot or something.

They could track people from small details like that if they collected enough of them.

Instead, Ronan waited for Hadley to turn the phone to him and show him the picture.

Ronan held in a groan as he did. The man had caught a small corner of the back of the car from the side. Not even a partial of the plate or a piece of a windshield where a registration might be. Nothing.

He watched as Hadley turned and showed the picture to Zach.

Zach hadn't schooled his expression as well as Ronan, and Hadley looked almost embarrassed.

"Sorry," he said turning the phone back to look at the picture himself again. "I guess it's not much."

"That's all right," Ronan said. "At least it's something. Any little bit of information is helpful." Or it could be someone visiting a neighbor across the street. Most of the leads they got in a case were just that. Something you hope might have meaning that turns out to be nothing. "Is there anything else?"

Ted Hadley shook his head.

"Okay. I need to get this information down as an official statement just in case it leads somewhere and we'll want to get that image from you. Give me a minute," he said, going to grab one of the junior detectives to take the report.

Ronan found three of the junior detectives in the break room bitching about the state of the coffee. They were still hopeful they could get the department to spring for better coffee if they all complained enough. Ronan knew better.

He opened his mouth to speak to one of them, but someone mentioned Tiff's name back in the bullpen.

"...name's Tiffany Carson, and she's one smart cookie."

Ronan shook his head, knowing Tiff would hate being referred to as a piece of food.

Jepsen. He was a colossal asshole and an arrogant know-it-all who thought he was hot stuff. And he was talking about Tiff.

Ronan growled and stepped around the corner of the break room to see Detective Jepsen leaning on his desk talking to a redheaded female officer who must have come up to the unit to drop something off and had the misfortune of being trapped by the resident jackass.

"She doesn't write the kind of true crime junk novels you can get in the bookstores. She's the real deal, a professor at a university. I'll be working with her on this cold case, letting her interview me for her latest book."

The officer looked like she knew exactly who Jepsen was, and by the way she was leaning away from him as he droned on, she wasn't buying his bullshit line.

Good for her. Jepsen had gotten the same directive they'd all gotten from Captain Calhoun to cooperate where they could with Tiff's research, but this dick was trying to turn it into a pickup line?

Ronan strode back to his desk where Ted Hadley sat waiting and smacked the pad of statement forms across Jepsen's chest, earning a satisfying, "oof," from the clown.

Zach was suppressing a grin as he stood and gathered his keys and wallet.

"Jepsen," he said, gesturing to Mr. Hadley in his seat, "Mr. Hadley needs to make a statement about something he saw related to the Barrett case. Zach and I have to look into a missing person report that might be connected to the case. Take Mr. Hadley's statement."

He didn't bother saying please. He outranked Jepsen, and although Ronan wasn't the kind of person to use his rank to push anyone around, he didn't like Jepsen even talking about Tiff, much less making it seem like they were close in some way.

It didn't even matter that he hadn't said anything bad about Tiffany. Ronan simply didn't like the way her name sounded leaving Jepsen's mouth.

Jepsen sneered and puffed out his chest, glancing at the officer he was trying to impress to be sure she was watching. "Get a junior detective to do it, Cafferty."

Ronan paused long enough to give Jepsen a hard stare before turning to Mr. Hadley. "Detective Jepsen is going to take down the details about the car you saw, and we'll follow up on it. Thank you for coming in today."

Jepsen groused, but he waved Hadley over to his own desk and sat down to complete the report.

Zach shared a grin with the redheaded officer on the way to the elevator, saying goodbye when she exited on the second floor as they continued to the ground level.

Ronan was still busy seething over Jepsen talking about his woman like that, but when he stepped outside the station, a cool breeze hit, feeling like a slap to the face.

His woman?

Had he really just thought that?

They'd had coffee together and they had plans for dinner that night, but he had no right to think of her so possessively.

He got into the car with Zach, moving on autopilot as he worked to shove back the feelings he was having for a woman he hardly knew. A woman who was clearly intelligent and passionate about her work and making a difference in the world. A woman he felt an intense attraction to that he couldn't shake and didn't want to. A woman who was on his mind much too much right now.

He shook himself. They had a missing man to find. Whatever was going on, he needed to get it figured out before the Barrett children wound up having to bury both their father and grandfather.

First the case.

He grinned. Then the woman.

CHAPTER 13

BY THE TIME RONAN AND ZACH REACHED NOAH BARRETT'S neighborhood, Luis Barrett still hadn't resurfaced. Patrol cars were visibly making the rounds in a six-block radius, slowing to check between houses and in parks, but there had yet to be any sightings.

At the house, standing along the front porch, the Barrett children were understandably distressed. The three of them looked toward Ronan and Zach with hopeful expressions when they arrived on the premises.

"Any news?" Nicole Barrett asked, her eyes darting from one detective to the other.

"We're working on it," Ronan said, thoroughly tired of having to tell people that. "Have you spoken with any of your neighbors?"

Nicole nodded. "I went to ask the neighbors myself if any of them had seen or heard Grandpa leave the house this morning. But none of them did." She pointed to the house to the left. "The guy who lives there said he might have heard a car door earlier, but he's not really sure. A random car door isn't something many people pay much attention to." She then pointed to the house on the right. "I spoke with them too, but they didn't hear or see anything."

Ronan nodded. "We're going to speak with them as well. In the meantime, can you call the home your grandfather lives in and tell them to be on the lookout for him in case he gets himself back there?"

Nicole nodded and her brother, Jeff, looked at Ronan.

"There are a few friends of Grandpa's that still live around here, I think. I'll see if I can track them down and let them know what's happening in case he reaches out to anyone."

The younger sister, Leslie, put a hand on her brother's arm, speaking quietly. "I'll help."

Minutes later, Ronan and Zach were standing in a neighbor's living room speaking to Mark Castle who appeared to be somewhere in his forties and lived alone.

"Can I get either of you anything to drink?" he asked.

"No, thank you," Zach replied. "But thanks for agreeing to speak with us."

"No problem." He folded his arms across his chest. "So, the poor old man is still missing, huh? That family has been through hell. It's not right."

Ronan couldn't argue with him. "His grandchildren say you heard a car door slam this morning?"

The man nodded and then rubbed the back of his neck. "Yeah, but honestly, that car door could have belonged to anyone. I'm not sure if it came from that direction or not," he said, tilting his head toward the right where the Barrett house stood. "I just vaguely remember hearing a car door slam at maybe six o'clock? It was still kind of dark outside and I had just gotten home from the night shift at the hospital."

Zach interjected. "You work at Yale New Haven?"

Castle nodded. "I'm an emergency room physician. I'm working night shifts this month."

Ronan recorded his notes before looking up from his pad. "You are aware that your neighbor Noah Barrett was found dead last week, correct?"

"Yeah, I know. I feel terrible for that family. They really are going through the wringer," he reiterated.

"Have you ever seen a black BMW next door?"

Mark looked upward to the ceiling, thinking. "I'm not sure. I do see the Audi of the woman across the street sometimes if she's making a quick stop and doesn't pull into her driveway."

They already had this man's statement about the time frame when Noah was missing, but Ronan wanted to see if he could offer anything else.

"Have you seen any other cars, maybe someone driving slowly through the neighborhood or a car that seemed to come around more than once?"

Mark shook his head. "No, I'm sorry. I don't remember. I mean, it's possible, but in all honesty, I tend to keep to myself and mind my own business. And from what I could tell, Noah was the same way."

"Well, thank you for your time, sir," Zach said.

"No problem."

As they left the house, Ronan could tell that Zach was just as frustrated as he was. Noah Barrett lived in a neighborhood where people took minding their own business to new heights.

Zach glanced sideways at Ronan. "I don't know. Maybe the grandfather's disappearance is unrelated. We have to consider that a possibility too, you know? Otherwise, we might miss something."

"True," Ronan said. The same thought had crossed his

mind and he was hoping the old man would turn up at a park or bus stop confused but safe.

Another one of their patrol cars cruised down the street, and Ronan and Zach both nodded at the uniformed officer inside.

In his periphery, Ronan saw Noah Barrett's two daughters return to the front porch, sentries hoping to spot Luis Barrett.

One of the main rules of being a detective was to not get too bogged down in a case. To not let it become personal. But as the hours and days ticked by, Ronan could feel himself becoming more invested and determined to not let the Barrett children down.

CHAPTER 14

Tiff crossed the parking lot at the college, dodging the potholes almost by memory, her notebooks and the eighteen stamped and addressed envelopes in her arms. She smiled at a student hurrying to his car, certain he was in her two-forty-six research course on Mondays and Wednesdays, but unable to remember his name.

"Tiff!"

She knew who was calling her before she saw him.

James Atkins had a greasy smile on his face as he edged up to her, a leather messenger bag slung across his shoulder and chest.

"James." She added a smile with the greeting but kept moving briskly toward her car.

Her momentum didn't bother him as he fell in step alongside her. "Did you hear the news?"

"I'm sure you'll tell me." Tiff knew without being told that whatever news he had would be about him. James wasn't a gossip unless the news he was spreading was somehow about himself.

His grin was instant, and he spun to step in front of her

so she could get the full-on effect of it when he stopped her in her tracks.

"I've been nominated for the Dearing."

Her shock probably registered on her face. The Bartholomew Rawley Dearing Award was granted by one of the largest historical associations in the United States, awarded annually to a historian recognized for their contribution to the work of American historians.

She wiped the shock from her face and smiled, this one a little more genuine. James was an ass and she didn't like him as a person, but his work was sound and even his nomination for the award brought prestige to the department. If he won, all the better.

"Congratulations, James. That's fantastic news." As she said the words, she had to admit she'd like saying them better if they were directed toward any of the other twenty-three professors in the department.

And as she wasn't an absolute saint, there was a twinge of jealousy hitting her in the moment, but she could be happy for her colleague all the same.

James moved toward her, reaching as if to take her stacks from her hands. "Come on. I'll carry those and we can go grab a drink."

Tiff pulled back. "Sorry, I have somewhere to be." And thank goodness for that. Much as she did think the nomination was impressive, she wasn't up for getting a drink with him.

He tossed his thumb over his shoulder in the general direction of the campus. "Really, you should come. A bunch of us are going to celebrate."

Tiff didn't know if there were really others going with him, but that didn't matter. She'd gone with him the first couple of times he told her the department was going for drinks. Sometimes, there were a few others there, but even if there were, he'd made it seem like she and he were arriving together and would be leaving together.

When she first arrived on campus, he'd fed rumors to that effect, much to her dismay. Since he outranked her in the department, she had to work overtime to get past the idea that she was a woman willing to sleep around to get where she wanted.

She'd begun being careful about putting up limits and boundaries, and no longer felt like she was battling that particular bit of gossip, but she wouldn't make that mistake again.

He stepped closer, putting his hands on her arms. "No, really, you should come."

Her arms were full so she couldn't raise them to push him back, but she didn't have to.

"Mrs. Carson?" Movement to her right accompanied the words, and Tiff turned to see a brown-haired man with creases at the corners of his eyes and a heavy dose of graying stubble on his chin.

The man looked uneasily between her and James like he wasn't sure if he should interrupt.

Shifting her burden in her arms, she turned and offered a smile. She wanted to get home, but this at least gave her an easy out with James.

"Congratulations, again, James," she said, offering a smile, but turning back to the new man right away so James didn't have an excuse to linger.

The man wasn't a student, or he would have called her professor or Doctor Carson, not Mrs. Carson. Not that she was the type to correct him. She only hoped he wasn't a parent of a student there to try to convince her to give a better grade to his son or daughter.

She might almost rather talk with James.

She was always amazed by the number of parents who thought it was okay to call and berate her for a grade they thought their child hadn't earned. She would tell him that same thing she told them all. That her policy on grades was firm. If a student hadn't come to see her for help or asked how they could bring up a grade on a test or paper before the deadline for grades, they'd missed their opportunity.

Instead, the man leaned closer, lowering his voice. "I'm sorry. I hope it was okay that I interrupted. You looked a little like you didn't want to be talking to that man."

Tiff relaxed and offered a small smile, glancing over her shoulder to be sure James was out of earshot. "Thank you. I appreciate that."

The man nodded, then held up one of her latest books. It was her third publication and one that had received high praise from her colleagues and peers, but that didn't explain why he was thrusting it at her.

"I did have another reason, though. I've just found your latest book and really enjoyed reading it."

Tiff nodded encouragingly, hoping to hurry the man to his point.

She only had a few more minutes to drop her letters in the mail if she wanted to make it home to shower before dinner with Ronan.

Which she did. She smiled, her chest fluttering again when she thought about seeing him. He turned out to be nothing like her first impression of him. Now that she knew he wasn't a cold bastard, she could focus on those sexy-as-sin looks and how when he smiled at her she felt like she'd won a prize, knowing she'd made him crack that serious veneer.

And he was dedicated and passionate about his job, his

mind working to piece together what had happened to tear someone's world apart so he could bring them justice and closure.

She realized with a jolt the man had been talking and she'd missed it. She focused on his words.

"Do you let people audit your classes?"

Ah, that's where he was going with this. She shifted her letters again, feeling the strap of her purse slip down her shoulder.

"Yes, you'll need to complete a form and bring it to me to sign before returning it to the registrar's office. There's a fee, but the registrar can explain all of that to you when you pick up the form."

His nod was enthusiastic. "Great, great. I'll go there now."

Tiff looked across the green grass of the quad. "I think they're closing in a few minutes, but if you hurry you might make it. It's just across campus in Hewett Hall."

The man nodded and stood watching her as she walked to her car. When she looked back, he raised a hand to wave and she wondered if he was watching her to be sure she got to her car without James coming back to harass her.

It was always a wonder to her how some men seemed to get it and others didn't. James would never see what he did as a problem. At least there were some men in the world who did.

She shrugged off all thoughts of James and let her mind drift back to Ronan. He was much more fun to think about and she found herself grinning the whole ride to the mailbox.

～

Ronan and Zach hadn't made much progress. After speaking with several more neighbors who didn't see anything and checking with hospitals and the church Noah Barrett attended, they were no closer to knowing where Luis Barrett had gone.

Back at the precinct, with a thick, black erasable marker in hand, Ronan added the name 'Luis Barrett' to the murder board in precise block letters, making a note of the time and date he went missing. He added a question mark to indicate the possibility it was linked to their case.

Ronan stepped back to examine the board, reflecting over everything they knew thus far—which unfortunately wasn't much. They were digging deep into Yasmine Bray's background and for the span of twenty minutes earlier in the day, they thought they'd linked her to one of the Massachusetts victims.

The letdown from the adrenaline rush once they figured out it was someone else with a similar name had left Ronan grumpy. That and the fact he hadn't grabbed enough to eat when they went through a drive-thru for lunch. He hated fast food.

"Hey there, detective," a voice drifted from behind him, sounding like soothing music to Ronan's ears on an exceptionally rough day.

He turned around and found Tiffany approaching, looking as luminous as ever. Her shiny black hair fell loose around her shoulders, and she was dressed in a white button-up blouse with black pants. Plain, but effortlessly gorgeous.

Was it seven o'clock already? How had that happened?

Ronan's mood kicked up at the sight of her, but he reminded himself that he was at work, and she was going to be interviewing several of his coworkers. She'd want him to keep their interaction professional.

He cleared his throat and resisted the urge to wrap his arms around her waist, instead only reaching out a hand to run it down her arm as he spoke low so no one would over-hear. "Hey, Tiff. I could get used to this planned break idea, since you're the one enforcing it."

She smiled tenderly, almost like she could tell their case wasn't going well. "How's it going?"

"It's going, I guess..." Ronan ran a hand through his hair, realizing he should change his shirt and comb his hair before they grabbed any food. He would take a quick break to eat with her and then bring back food for the other detec-tives on the team.

The Thai place let the department order family-sized portions at a discount when they were working overtime.

"Any new developments?" Tiff glanced at the board behind him.

"If by new developments you mean new problems, then yes." He stepped closer to her, hands still itching to reach out to her. "The father of our victim went missing this morning. We don't know if his disappearance is related, or if the poor man just got confused and wandered off some-where. His grandkids said he was already in a frail state, and the news of his son dying certainly didn't help matters."

"Oh geez. I'm sorry," Tiff said, then squinted as she looked closely at the board with a furrowed brow.

Ronan moved to step in front of it. He shouldn't be letting her examine their work on an active case so carefully, but before he could, her face cleared and she looked to him, eyes round.

"Oh, wow..." She looked back to the board, a light bulb clearly going off in her head.

Ronan studied her. "What is it?"

"These names." She looked at him again and put her hand to his chest to move him aside. "Are these people all linked to your case?" She didn't wait for an answer. "They're all related to the Howell case!"

"The who?" Zach came up behind them, returning with pages he'd printed from their social media search of Marcus Jones and Yasmine Bray.

Ronan searched his memory for the name 'Howell' but came up blank.

Tiff met his gaze and spoke excitedly. "The Addie and Teddy Howell case happened forty years ago. I researched the case as part of my dissertation when I got my doctorate. They were teenaged siblings from Springfield, Mass-achusetts. Addie was sixteen and Teddy was fourteen. On the outside, theirs was a picture-perfect middle-class family. But in 1981, they murdered their parents in their sleep."

Ronan's jaw tightened knowing there was a lot more to that picture-perfect family. "What was going on behind closed doors?"

Zach set down his papers and circled to stand beside Ronan as Tiff relayed details.

"Nothing good, as you can imagine. Addie claimed her father had been raping her from the age of eleven. Even worse, her mother allegedly knew about it but didn't inter-vene, pretending it wasn't happening. Addie and Teddy had two younger siblings, one of them a girl who had just turned ten. The teens' story was that Addie worried their father would turn to the younger girl and they were determined to make sure that never happened. Addie and Teddy slit their parents' throats in their sleep."

Throats slit. An image of Noah Barrett's dead body flashed into Ronan's mind. "Teenagers did that?" Ronan asked, trying to wrap his mind around the kind of rage and pain that would have taken.

Tiff nodded, seemingly understanding his skepticism. "Addie hit their father in the head with a hammer several times to keep him down while Teddy cut the mom's throat and then later the father's, though Addie's beating had already taken his life."

Zach looked at the names on their murder board. "And what do these names have to do with that case."

There was now a small gathering of other detectives around them and the energy buzzing around them said they all knew they were about to move forward on this case in a huge way.

Tiff pointed at the board. "Noah Barrett was their neighbor back then. He was sixteen at the time. The police interviewed him, and he said Addie and Teddy had an unusual brother-sister relationship. Said they were a little *too* close."

Ronan turned his gaze to the board, staring at Noah Barrett's name. Could this all really go back to a case that happened when Barrett was a kid?

"Noah's father, Luis Barrett," Tiff continued, "represented the kids in court."

Ronan blinked, shocked. "Really? That kind of thing wouldn't fly nowadays if his son had given the investigators information."

Tiff pointed at him with an approving nod and he could picture her doing the same with a student in her class.

"True. But things were different back then. Luis Barrett volunteered to represent the kids, and since no one objected, the court allowed it. Anyway, it's not widely known that Noah Barrett made any statements to the police. I only found that out when I met with someone who'd been around during the initial investigation. Noah never testified because he didn't have anything truly significant to add to the already overwhelming evidence."

"Did you ever publish your findings?"

Tiff shook her head. "I was going to but changed my mind. It wasn't right for the piece I was working on at the time, so I just filed it away, planning to use it for something later. The information is out there though if you look hard enough."

"What about the others?" Ronan asked, gesturing to the Massachusetts victims.

"Gretchen Meyer was a caseworker in the 1980s. She was assigned to look into allegations Addie made against her father to one of her teachers. She closed the case though, after interviewing the Howell family and their neighbors. She didn't believe Addie's claims were credible and referred her for counseling. She left social work after the Howells killed their parents."

"She went to work in a doctor's office, so we didn't find a connection between her and Acavedo." Zach looked grim as he relayed the information.

"You couldn't know," Tiff said. "She was never called to testify or even interviewed in the case. I found her years later when I looked into the allegation Addie had made."

"The kids' attorney didn't call her to testify in their defense?" Ronan was shocked. A good defense attorney should have been raising exigent circumstances and making sure the sexual abuse came out.

Tiff shook her head, her expression saying it all. She thought the case had been botched as well.

She pointed to the other name on the board. "William Acavedo was the prosecutor. Even though Addie was only sixteen, Acavedo tried her as an adult and made her out to be the leader in planning the murders. Teddy was deemed to be just following her orders and he was tried separately as a juvenile. When it was all said and done, Addie was sent to prison, where she died in a knife fight at the age of nineteen."

Ronan almost shuddered. Addie's case was so tragic, he wondered why he hadn't heard of it before. He shook his head. "And what happened to the other siblings?"

"The two younger siblings were placed into foster care. Teddy was sentenced to juvenile detention until he was eighteen. There are records of him getting arrested several times after that though, for things like burglary and assault. The last record I found showed he was released after serving two years on an assault charge in 2000. After that, he just kind of fell off the grid."

Ronan's mind worked to fit the latest puzzle pieces together. It wasn't completely clear just yet, but it looked like their killer was getting revenge against anyone involved in the Howell case.

CHAPTER 15

Tiff promised to check her notes on the Howell case and Ronan promised to take her to dinner as soon as the case ended. As much as he wanted more time with her, now that they had a direction, there would be no breaks. No time for anything other than the case.

Ronan looked across his desk toward Zach who was murmuring something as he scrolled through something on the screen of his computer.

"What is it?" Ronan asked.

"The judge in the Howell case died of a heart attack ten years ago. The medical examiner fifteen years ago in a car accident. I was just wondering if their deaths might be linked, even though the causes don't match up to what this killer is doing now."

Ronan stood and approached the board, adding the names of the judge and medical examiner with the cause of death next to each name. His gut said they weren't linked to the case.

He turned back to Zach. "I don't know. I could maybe

buy the car accident if our killer hadn't worked up to close-up-and-personal killing yet, but not the heart attack. This isn't a killer with the sophistication to pull that off."

Zach tipped his head to the side. "I don't know. They're sophisticated enough that they aren't leaving much trace evidence behind."

Ronan shook his head. "Not the same thing as knowing how to induce a heart attack or make a death look like a heart attack and get your hands on the right kind of substances to make that happen. It's too clean. This killer is brutal and angry. More than that. They're filled with rage and they aren't holding back."

"What do you think the odds are of Teddy being behind all of this?" Zach asked. "Forty years later, and still ticked off about the Barretts' role in their case?"

The possibility had crossed Ronan's mind. Teddy was a key player in the initial murders and he probably harbored a lot of anger over his sister's conviction and subsequent death. "I don't understand why he would start killing again now though, after all these years. Why such a long wait? Wouldn't he have gone after them shortly after Meyer and Acavedo?"

Zach met his gaze. "Maybe not if he wanted to avoid getting caught? Then again, remember the Kenworth case. Sometimes, there's an unexpected twist."

That was definitely a good point.

Ronan thought about Luis Barrett and he knew there was very little chance he was simply lost.

If he was currently being held captive, how much longer would he have before their killer tired of him? Noah had been abducted Friday, but it had taken two days for the murderer to finish him off. Did Luis still have a couple days?

Would he be able to withstand the kind of beating Noah had with his already failing health?

Zach's phone rang. He answered the call and placed it on speaker. "Detective Reynolds speaking."

"Hello, detective. This is dispatch. We have a caller reporting a sighting of a man fitting the description of Luis Barrett."

"Where?" Zach asked, while Ronan listened, pen in hand to take down the information.

Minutes later, the two of them were in their car, heading to the location with uniformed officers accompanying them.

Ronan's heart pounded as the warehouse came into view —a large, abandoned building, partially boarded up, with busted windows. Graffiti covered the outer walls.

When they'd parked, Ronan gave quick instructions to the other officers, sending two to cover any back entrances as he and Zach and the others stacked in formation, each standing behind another angled at the right shoulder of the person in front of them.

Moving quickly as a unit, they approached the warehouse, making their way to the door.

Zach and Ronan in the lead, they listened but heard nothing. Ronan radioed the officers at the back.

"We've got eyes through an open window back here," the officer at the back responded in a low voice. "One body down, no sign of anyone else that we can see."

"Breach on three," Ronan said to both his team and the pair at the back.

They were too late.

"Dammit!" Zach roared, voicing what Ronan was feeling.

Luis Barrett's body was crumpled in a heap on the floor not ten feet from the entrance. Beaten, bloodied...dead.

Ronan's heart sank, the faces of Noah Barrett's three children swimming in his head. They might be adults, but that didn't matter. They shouldn't have to bury their father and grandfather so close together.

This wasn't how Luis Barrett's case was supposed to end. They were supposed to bring the old man home. Blood was still pooling from the slash at his neck, and his eyes were wide open, showcasing the fear he'd felt during his last moments.

Ronan carefully approached and knelt, feeling for a pulse.

He shook his head at Zach and the others.

The body was still warm though.

Ronan stood and yelled, "Search the premises and fan out to search the grounds! Whoever did this might be close!"

The uniforms sprang into action, sending the warehouse into a frenzy. Minutes later, more uniforms arrived, along with search dogs. They swarmed the area, searching every inch of the warehouse and the grounds surrounding it.

But after an hour, it was obvious the killer had escaped. Ronan couldn't wrap his mind around how they had gotten so close, only to fall short. It just didn't make sense. Whoever was behind these murders was practically a ghost, constantly disappearing into thin air.

Ronan leaned against one of the squad cars, wallowing in his disappointment as Zach came over and stopped beside him, equally disappointed.

"This slippery, murdering bastard," Zach muttered. He hung his head. "Someone has to tell the Barrett kids."

Ronan's stomach churned at the thought, but he wasn't going to shirk away from facing them. "I'll do it. You stay here with the forensics team. Our killer obviously left in a hurry. Maybe he left something behind this time around."

Maybe their killer had gotten messy and they'd catch a break this time.

CHAPTER 16

RONAN WAS SURVIVING ON COFFEE AND ADRENALINE AT THIS point, and it was the shit coffee from the precinct to boot. He'd spent an hour the night before with the Barretts, every minute feeling like he was drowning in the agonizing sorrow that was their existence for the foreseeable future.

He and Zach were both back in the bullpen after getting no more than a couple hours sleep for the night, waiting for the analysis from the crime scene technicians to come through.

The overly acidic coffee was eating through his gut and he pulled open his drawer, digging for a granola bar to try to offset the effect on his empty stomach.

Zach raised both hands one on top of the other as though he were catching a baseball, a gesture that meant he wanted one too. Ronan tossed a bar his way before unwrapping his and eating half of it in one bite.

They ate in silence, ignoring the other detectives in the unit for the moment.

Minutes later their wait ended as Stephanie Kyler, one of the technicians from the forensics team, entered and beelined it to their desks, her short afro pulled away from her face in a headband and her dark skin looking sallow with exhaustion.

Ronan knew she and many of the other people who ran the lab and collected evidence for the major crimes division were working overtime on this case as well. And with this one, the frustration level was high given how little they had found at each of the scenes.

"Anything?" Zach asked.

"Not much. We did find two hairs on the body this time that don't belong to the victim, but they didn't contain any roots."

Zach sighed. "No roots, no DNA. Dammit."

"Anything else that might help us catch this..." Ronan stopped himself from saying what he'd wanted to say. The captain had come out of his office and was listening to the report Stephanie was giving them.

It might only cost him a dollar if he swore, but to Ronan that wasn't the point. He didn't like letting anyone see him lose control of his emotions. He'd learned a long time ago to keep his emotions in check and, when he couldn't, to hide them well. It had started with the kids who bullied him as a kid, and then with the teachers who told him time and time again he wasn't good enough.

Old habits die hard, and he still kept a tight rein on his emotions, allowing himself to feel them but keeping them below the surface where others couldn't see.

"There are new techniques," Stephanie offered hesitantly, "where we might be able to extract DNA from the hair itself, even without the roots."

Ronan was familiar with the technique, but he also knew that method was incredibly expensive and not widely used because most departments couldn't afford it and there was no guarantee yet that a court would accept the results.

Theirs was no exception. They didn't even have the necessary technological equipment for it. "We don't have the funds or the tech for that."

Stephanie was nodding. "You're right about that, but maybe we can ask the state lab?"

Ronan offered her a tired smile. "We can always try, but I doubt they can get us anything quickly, even if they are willing to try." Ronan knew there were only a handful of cases where judges had accepted the new science, and even then the defendants were appealing on the basis that the science was unreliable.

"I'm sorry, detectives. If you find us a suspect, we can at least match hair samples."

Ronan nodded. "Thanks."

Stephanie left and Ronan sat back in his seat, eyeing the coffee cup on his desk but dismissing the idea of another cup. He needed the energy jolt, but he couldn't stomach any more of it.

Zach flopped back down into his seat. "If we ever get our hands on this murderer, I feel like I might kill him myself."

"Hey, don't say that out loud," Ronan said before spotting Tiff entering the bullpen, an officer at her side again.

He stood to greet her and this time, he drew her out into the hall, moving them so they were covered behind an open door.

He put his hands to her waist and pulled her close, watching her face for her reaction to his touch.

She gave him exactly what he was looking for. Her cheeks flushed and she licked her lips as she let him pull her close, her body relaxing into him.

Another glance at the hall behind them told him they

were still alone. "I want you to know, I really want to see you when this is all over. I want to see where this might go between us. Hell, I want to make sure this does go somewhere between us because I really like you, teacher or not."

He was finished trying to pretend this would be a short fling. It would be anything but that if he had his way.

"Teacher or not?" she asked, her tone chilling a bit as she gave him that raised-brow look that probably made her students squirm.

"Sorry, that came out wrong," he said, hurrying to explain. "After the way my teachers treated me growing up, I've always had a thing against teachers. I didn't date them. Ever. But you're different."

"Mm-hmm." She put enough sarcasm into those two little sounds to tell him he was screwing this all up.

He opened his mouth, trying to figure out what to say to smooth this over, but she let him off the hook.

"It's okay, Ronan. I get it. When I first met you, I saw the way your attention dropped the second you knew what I did for a living. I made some assumptions myself, thinking you must be one of those guys who didn't like smart women. Someone who needed to feel superior to the women he dated. I've seen too many of those men so I jumped to conclusions."

"I'm sorry you have to deal with that," Ronan said, squeezing his hands on her waist.

"Yeah, well, it's reality and I've learned to deal with it, but I'm glad I took the time to see that you're not like them."

Ronan grinned. "I am too. So, a full-on date when this is over? One where I pick you up at your place and take you out to a nice restaurant and then walk you to your door when it's over?"

He leaned down, letting his lips brush hers with only the

barest hint of contact. "One where I get to kiss you goodnight."

Her breath caught and the caveman in him grew ten sizes at her reaction.

Tiff ran a hand up his chest to his shoulder. "I'd like that."

"Good." Ronan had to force himself to step back from her, knowing he had to cool his body's reaction to her before he went back to his desk. "You had something for us?"

"Oh!" she nodded. "I looked at my notes on the Howell case for you," she informed. "Other than the crime scene technicians and the police officers who testified, the other main person involved was a psychologist who testified that Addie was sane and understood the consequences of her actions. This, of course, negated the insanity plea Addie's lawyers had been pushing. Her name is Sheila Taylor, and she currently lives in Hartford, Connecticut."

Too close for comfort. Their killer could easily make the trip to Hartford. "Thank you so much, Tiff. I owe you."

He watched her leave before returning to the bullpen to grab his partner and the keys to their SUV. "We need to get to Hartford. Tiff says there's a psychiatrist there who testified that Addie Howell was sane and fully understood the consequences of her actions when she killed her parents."

He pointed at Jepsen, the closest detective with nothing on his plate. "Get a number for a Dr. Sheila Taylor in Hartford and see if you can get her on the phone. She might be our killer's next victim!"

Zach stood, pulling out his cell as they moved. "I'll call Hartford PD and have them send a car then have Shauna meet us there."

Hartford was outside their jurisdiction but Shauna was a state police officer. The whole damned state was her playground and they knew she'd be more than happy to lend a hand.

They hit the road with lights and sirens blasting. Shauna would beat them there since she was stationed up in Hartford, but that was okay. It would mean she'd be able to secure the doctor in less than ten minutes instead of the forty it would take Ronan and Zach to arrive.

Ronan's phone rang and Zach answered it on speaker.

"It's Jepsen," came the voice, and Ronan had to give the man credit. When shit hit the fan, even Jepsen got serious. "No answer on either the doctor's personal line or her office. I'll keep trying."

"Thanks, Jep," Zach said, ending the call before dialing into Hartford's dispatch.

As Ronan navigated the roads, the dispatch operator kept them updated. Doctor Taylor's office was closed and there were no signs of a disturbance.

"Officers are en route to her home now," the operator relayed.

Ronan and Zach listened in silence to several minutes of dead air.

"There's no answer at her home," the operator said.

"We have reason to believe she's in imminent danger," Ronan said, urging them to go in.

"I've let them know that, sir," the operator said, and Ronan resisted the urge to punch the steering wheel. He hated not being able to be there, to make the call himself so that at least if something happened, he knew he'd done everything he could to prevent someone from coming to harm.

He could hear the back and forth on the radio between dispatch and the Hartford officers.

"They're entering the premises, sir," said the operator.

Ronan held his breath as Zach did the opposite, letting his out in a whoosh beside him. Ronan would breathe easy when they had word the doctor was safe.

There was noise then in the background and Ronan thought he heard screaming, but as they were listening in to the operator's call with the officers, it wasn't at all clear.

After moments that seemed to drag on, Ronan heard the operator again. "They've got her. The doctor was safe. Just got a nice surprise from our uniforms interrupting her shower."

"Oops," Zach quipped, but Ronan didn't care.

The woman would probably be pissed off or confused or frightened, but that didn't matter. They'd seen what this killer was capable of and getting caught in the shower was nothing compared to how things could have ended.

When they arrived on scene in front of a small white house with light blue shutters, Shauna was sitting on a couch in the living room with a woman with steely gray hair cut short and large blue eyes.

The woman was dressed in a green sweater and black pants, but her hair was wet, and she looked tired. No, haggard was more like it.

Then again, the kind of morning she'd just had might do that to a person.

Hartford police officers stood nearby. Captain Calhoun had arranged with their captain to have them remain on site with the doctor until they were sure she wasn't in danger.

Once Shauna had introduced Ronan and Zach, she explained that she had already let the doctor know they thought someone related to an old case might be trying to harm her.

Zach took the lead in questioning her. "Do you

remember the homicide case involving Addie and Teddy Howell, about forty years ago?"

A haunted expression formed in her eyes. "Of course, I remember. A case like that sticks with you." She frowned as she wrapped her arms around herself and looked up at them. "Someone should have stopped it from happening."

Ronan watched the woman and thought he saw self-recrimination there.

He wondered if there was a reason for that. "Can you tell us how you became involved in the case?"

Dr. Taylor was slow to answer and seemed far away for a moment before shaking herself. "I had begun to see Addie Howell several weeks before the murders."

Ronan took that in. Had Addie said something that the doctor later thought should have told her she was going to beat and murder her parents in their sleep?

Dr. Taylor continued. "I should have seen what was happening, but I didn't."

"It's our understanding that you didn't believe Addie Howell was insane?" Zach asked. "Your testimony is part of what landed her in prison."

Dr. Taylor nodded, pressing her hands together tightly in her lap, slow to answer again, as though she was conflicted about telling them what had happened. "That's correct. I testified that Addie was aware of her actions and of the consequences of those actions. That she met the legal definition of sane."

"You're aware she died in prison?"

The woman's eyes softened and genuine sorrow crossed her face. "I am. It was horrible."

"What about her brother, Teddy Howell?" Ronan asked. "Have you heard from him since the trial?"

The woman's brows pinched and she shook her head.

"They're both dead," she said after a moment. "Teddy died from a drug overdose several years ago. I don't remember what year, but I'm sure of it. Like I said, I won't ever forget that case or those kids. Addie might not have met the definition of insane, but they were both very troubled. I don't believe for a minute that their parents hadn't put them through some kind of hell as children."

Ronan stopped writing in his notepad in midsentence.

Teddy was dead?

He glanced at Zach, who looked just as stunned by the news as Ronan was.

If Teddy was dead, so was their theory that he was the killer they were looking for.

And if he wasn't behind the murders, who was? Who else would hold a vendetta against those who testified against Addie Howell in court?

Dr. Taylor looked at each of the detectives in turn, fingering the sleeve of her sweater. "Is there anything else I can answer for you?"

Ronan shook his head. They needed to regroup. "No. That will be all, ma'am. Thank you for your time."

He gestured and the Hartford police officers came forward to explain their protection detail to her.

When he heard her trying to brush it off, Ronan moved back to her. "Ma'am, I can't stress enough how violent this killer is."

The doctor flinched, stepping back, and Ronan's stomach clenched at the idea of frightening her, but she needed to understand.

"He's not just killing his victims. He's torturing them first and taking pleasure in it. You need to let us keep you safe until we find whoever's doing this."

The dark circles under her eyes seemed to grow even

more prominent, emphasizing her haunted gaze, but she nodded.

As they stood outside their car minutes later, Shauna looked back at the house. "I take it that you guys didn't know Teddy Howell was dead?"

Zach sighed. "Yeah. Just a little something that seems to have escaped our awareness." He shook his head. "Every step forward we make with this case ends up setting us two steps back. This is ridiculous."

Ronan folded his arms across his chest, his mind puzzling out possibilities. "Maybe we aren't too far off. We know Addie and Teddy have two other siblings, and that Addie and Teddy claimed they were worried their father might abuse the sister. What if he already did before they could stop him? What if the younger sister is the one looking for vengeance for the siblings who tried to protect her?"

"Or the younger brother," Shauna interjected. "He might think his siblings were treated unfairly and want revenge?"

"Looks like we need to shift our attention to the youngest Howells, then," Zach said.

Ronan agreed. They needed to figure out where the younger siblings went and if they might be following in the murderous footsteps of the older Howells.

CHAPTER 17

TIFF HAD ALTERED HER LESSON PLAN THAT MORNING AT THE last minute, deviating from the syllabus in her Craft and Business of the Historian course.

Her mind had been on the families of Herschel Kenworth's victims and the letters she'd written them, as well as on the Howell children, now that Ronan's case had dredged up her research from that horrific crime.

So instead of lecturing on archival primary sources, she was discussing personal interviews of the subject of a historical event, specifically interviewing the survivors of violent crime.

She turned and walked to the other side of the space at the front of the small lecture hall. Moving as she taught had been a habit of hers from her second day of teaching. On day one, she'd tried to stand behind a lectern and nearly made herself crazy clutching the sides of it to keep herself in place.

When the class left, she gave herself a firm talking to and told herself not to try to fit a mold she'd somehow picked out in her head. From the next class on, she'd begun using all the space given to her at the front of the classroom.

"Sadly, there is no foolproof way to engage with survivors or relatives of the victims of a crime. What you have to remember is that you're seeking to bring these people back to the worst day of their lives in many cases. It's often something they either haven't been able to move beyond and are haunted by, or they've worked incredibly hard to move past it with therapy and support, and you want to drag them back to it."

She moved to the center of the room and looked out on the class, laying out the various ways she'd found of reaching out and what had worked best for her, before pausing to look down at her notes. She talked about giving them a reason to speak with you and about accepting "no" if that was someone's answer.

She looked up and laced her fingers together in front of her. "Now, what do you do when you've gotten a 'yes' from someone and you're sitting down to talk?"

She discussed choosing a location, setting the person at ease, offering tissues and water, and explaining ground rules.

"Ask permission to record the session and let them know that unless they tell you otherwise, you may use what they tell you in your research, book, or other media. Give them permission to turn off the recording any time they want to and nothing they say during that time will be used."

She paused and raised her hands, palms up. "Then, you let them talk. This is their trauma. It's their experience and you need to honor that and let them tell it to you in their way."

A student in the fourth row raised her hand.

Tiff pointed at her with a nod.

The dark-haired girl's brows came together. "Then how do you make sure you get what you need?"

"There's an art to it. You begin by asking an open question that doesn't guide or restrict them. Something along the lines of, 'What would you like to share with me about the night XYZ crime happened,' or, 'I've read the accounts of XYZ but I can't claim that gives me any true understanding of your experience. Would you be willing to tell me some of your feelings and memories about XYZ?'"

Tiff moved across the room, then turned and moved back again, thinking about her experiences with survivors and their families.

"In the beginning, many of the people you interview will be hesitant. They'll say something and then ask if what they said was okay, or if that's what you're looking for. You can set them at ease by explaining that you don't have a set agenda. That you want to learn whatever they're willing to share."

The same girl replied, "But I will have an agenda. There will be certain things I need, won't there?"

Tiff smiled. "True, but everything the person tells you is of potential value so your goal in the beginning is simply to get them speaking. As the interview continues, you can begin to probe deeper into areas you're hoping for more on, but all of it needs to be done with respect and care. If you exacerbate the trauma the person has gone through, you're no longer a historian seeking answers, you're part of their suffering."

The girl nodded and Tiff looked around the rest of the room. She saw nodding heads from several students. She saw the usual handful of kids who looked like they were checked out or too tired from partying to pay attention. She wasn't their mother. It was up to them to work or not.

In the back row along the left side of the room was the

man who'd stopped her in the parking lot. He'd caught the registrar before they left the previous day and had come to her this morning with the necessary paperwork to audit the course.

He was hoping to write a family history and wanted to audit the course to understand what resources he might use to learn more personal history about the family members he'd tracked during his genealogy research.

She gave him a nod before continuing, her gaze returning to the girl who'd originally asked the question. "Keep in mind, also, that you don't need to get all your answers at once. You can ask your subject if it's okay to reach out again if you have other questions. Or, you can stop the interview if your subject is struggling and suggest meeting again to finish it at a later date, though I suggest not waiting too long between sessions. Schedule something for three to four days out if you can."

She looked to the clock and saw the period was ending. "That's all for today. Since I moved around the schedule, check your syllabus for the assigned reading. There are three articles, all on reserve in the library for you." She raised her voice to speak over the scuffling of feet and closing of books as people began to pack up. "And be sure to read the description of next week's class so you're prepared for what we're doing. I want all of you to come in knowing ahead of time what to expect."

She'd be showing them an interview with a kidnapping survivor Tiff had interviewed multiple times. The woman was incredible, not only overcoming the trauma she'd endured after she escaped her captor, but after several years had passed, she'd allowed Tiff to use the taped interviews in classes.

Days when she showed those videos, each and every

student would be awake and focused. She always gave people a warning both on the syllabus and in class ahead of time. She'd also send an email later in the week, but for now, she packed her notes away and gathered the blazer she'd shed during her lecture.

Today was her half day on campus and she wanted to see if she could find anything more in her notes that might help Ronan and Zach stop the killer they were chasing. If there was anything she could do to ensure there would be fewer victims or family members for a future historian to research, she'd do it.

CHAPTER 18

"ANY CHANCE TIFF HAS ANYTHING MORE FOR US?" ZACH asked, looking up from his computer.

They'd spent the morning working on the red tape necessary to get the Commonwealth of Massachusetts to release information about the remaining Howell siblings to them. So far as they knew, both siblings had gone into the foster care system, but getting information on where they went from there meant a lot of legwork to obtain orders from a Massachusetts judge to allow them access.

Ronan took out his phone and checked for messages. Not that he hadn't already checked that day. He'd checked plenty. He had called Tiff the day before to let her know they'd secured the doctor and that Teddy Howell was already dead.

Of course, he'd used the excuse to talk to her longer than he strictly had to, asking about her day and what her plans for dinner were. He couldn't wait to be able to take her on a real date.

The chemistry was there between them, and he was attracted to her sharp mind and her passion for what she did. He was willing to bet when they were able to focus on them without the case to keep pulling him away, there would be fireworks between them and then some.

He sent her a quick message. *Checking to see if you found anything more in your notes. Hitting a dead end here and hoping you'll be our ace in the hole again.*

"This case is starting to get on my nerves," Zach said.

"Well, it's already been on mine," Ronan scoffed.

There were other leads they could potentially check into, such as the black BMW the contractor reported seeing. Yet, the more Ronan thought about those other leads, the more insignificant they now seemed.

Maybe it was just intuition, but he felt pretty certain that they now needed to keep their focus on the Howell family. There was no way the person committing the crimes didn't have a tie to this family.

"What about the parents?" he asked. "We shouldn't just be looking at the Howells as a nuclear family. Let's branch out and see what we can find."

Zach frowned. "I guess I've just assumed if the two younger siblings went into foster care, that meant there were no other surviving family members."

Ronan had to admit, Zach had a point, but they couldn't make assumptions like that. "Still, let's be sure."

Zach nodded. "Do you want to follow up with that and I'll touch base with the uniformed officers who were canvasing Noah Barrett's neighbors to see if they found any more information on the black BMW the contractor saw?"

"Works for me," Ronan said, opening up a computer screen to see what he could find out on the rest of the Howell family.

Before he started, though, he checked his phone again for any news from Tiff. His disappointment to find he had no messages or calls felt way too close to the upset he'd felt when he was waiting for Amy Mann to call him after he gave her his phone number in seventh grade. He was falling for Tiff Carson and falling hard.

And he didn't care one bit.

CHAPTER 19

TWO HOURS LATER, RONAN HAD FOUND OUT JUST HOW isolated the Howell kids had been. Neither had living grandparents and the only siblings were a brother of Mrs. Howell who had died two years before the Howell murders and a sister of Mr. Howell who'd been estranged from the family for years.

Zach had turned up a juvenile record on Yasmine Bray involving an incident where she cut another student with a knife during a fight in junior high school. She was put on probation and the record was sealed, but Zach had been able to get a judge to open the record for them.

It was that record that had brought them back to Yasmine Bray's office where she looked at them with what seemed like wearing patience.

"What can I do for you?" she said politely from behind her desk.

"Thanks again for your willingness to talk to us," Ronan prefaced. He cleared his throat. "We're here about your juvenile record."

Ms. Bray's brows went up. "You mean the sealed record?"

"We were able to have a judge open it in light of the nature of the crimes we're investigating."

She frowned at Ronan's words. "Crimes? Has there been another murder?"

Ronan would have thought she would have seen the news and he studied her to see if he sensed any guile. Would she have a reason to pretend not to know about Noah Barrett's father?

While Ronan was watching her, Zach answered her question.

"Noah Barrett's father was kidnapped and killed in much the same manner as Noah."

Yasmine went white. If she was faking it, she was damned good.

"Your juvenile arrest involved you stabbing another student at your school?" Ronan pushed.

Yasmine seemed to startle out of her shock, and she made a face of disgust. "Stabbing is an enormous stretch. I was in junior high and I kissed the wrong boy. Or rather, he kissed me. Turns out he was dating another girl. She came after me in shop class, tackling me and pulling my hair and stuff."

"Where does the knife come in?" Zach asked.

Ms. Bray shook her head. "Not a knife. A craft blade I'd been using to trim around the edge of a piece of foam for a project. When she tackled me, the blade sliced her arm and she said I'd stabbed her."

She made a face. "I was a foster kid so there wasn't really anyone to stand up for me. The home I was in at the time wasn't really a June Cleaver kind of home. But the girl who jumped me was wealthy. Her parents knew how to put up a stink and they did it. I was arrested. She got detention."

Ronan sat forward. "You were in the foster care system?"

He studied her. Was there any possibility she was the younger Howell sibling? She could be around the right age, but he hadn't looked at her birth date carefully before, so it was hard to say. She was younger than Noah Barrett, he thought.

If memory served, the younger Howell girl would have been six or seven years younger than Noah, so that seemed plausible. Could she be Teddy Howell's sister? Would she have tracked down Noah Barrett and seduced him to get close enough to him to enact some kind of revenge?

She nodded. "I was. And when I was arrested for that fight, I ended up getting probation and community service. I did my community service at a local charity and ended up meeting my adoptive mom and dad there. It ended up being a blessing."

Zach must have been thinking the same thing as Ronan was because he asked, "Do you know anything about your birth parents?"

Ms. Bray's face registered surprise and then irritation. "I'm at a loss as to what this has to do with your investigation."

"We're just trying to check a few links between the victims and it's possible one of the links might be their time in foster care. Anything you can tell us would be helpful."

She didn't look like she was buying it entirely, but she answered despite the scowl on her face. "My adoption was a closed adoption. The only thing I know is that my parents died when I was an infant."

Ronan jotted down her explanation. If she was the younger Howell daughter, she would have been orphaned when she was ten years old, not an infant. Of course, if she was the Howell daughter and was involved in their current homicides, she'd have every reason to lie.

They would need to try to open her records.

"Okay. And one last thing..." Ronan glanced upward from his notes. "Where were you in the summer of 1981?"

"Really, detectives?" she said dryly.

"If you have a general idea?" Ronan said. He wanted to know if she was in the area when the Massachusetts killings began.

She paused for a minute, holding his gaze before smiling. "Actually, I can tell you exactly where I was. I was in Turkey. I worked for a nonprofit organization that helped child refugees from 1980 to 1983."

"And there are records of this?"

She nodded. "There should be, but I don't think I have any."

They got the name of the organization to follow up and thanked her for her time.

"What do you think?" Ronan asked as he and Zach left the building.

"I think we absolutely need to make sure every word of her story checks out."

"Agreed," Ronan said, getting into the passenger seat as Zach got behind the wheel.

They'd only gone two blocks when Zach's phone rang. He jerked his head toward his phone. "Put it on speaker, would you?"

When Ronan did, Shauna spoke, not bothering with anything by way of a greeting for Zach. "Are you with Ronan, Zach?"

Her tone set Ronan on edge. "I'm here," he said, loud enough for the phone to pick up as he and Zach shared a concerned look.

"Have you talked to Tiff today?" Shauna didn't sound

panicked, but she didn't sound normal either. There was a little too much casual to her voice.

Ronan's heart stuttered. "Not since last night. I tried calling but haven't gotten an answer. She was teaching this morning, though. I just figured she was still in class or tied up on campus."

"Baby, what's wrong?" Zach asked, briefly taking his eyes off the road to glance at the phone with worry.

"We were supposed to go out for lunch," Shauna explained, "but when I got to her place to pick her up, she wasn't there. Her apartment door was open, and that's not like her. And even though nothing looked out of place, her car, purse, and phone were all still there."

The blood drained from Ronan's veins, leaving him cold.

Zach went immediately on alert. "No signs of a struggle?"

"Correct," Shauna replied, "but I don't have a good feeling about this."

Ronan knew Shauna was a good cop. She had the experience to know when something wasn't right and he trusted her gut.

"Could she have gone for a walk and thought the door latched behind her but didn't? She wouldn't take her purse on a walk," Zach offered.

Ronan spoke over the slamming of his heart in his chest. "She'd take her phone, though."

Shauna didn't speak.

"We're on our way," Zach said, hitting the sirens and lights.

CHAPTER 20

Tiff groaned, pain batting at the sides of her head as her stomach pitched, nausea creeping up her throat. She felt sluggish and stiff, somehow knowing something wasn't right, but not at all sure what that meant.

One minute, she thought she could grasp the warning floating through her head and make sense of it, and then it was gone and she was left in a dizzying loop of confusion.

She must be sick. She remembered coming home from campus. Had she gotten in bed? Was she running a fever?

No, she wasn't in a bed. She was sitting up. She attempted to lift her hand to rub at her temples but couldn't. In fact, she couldn't move her arms at all.

Somewhere deep inside her, warning bells rang and she knew in that moment she needed to open her eyes. She needed to know what was happening, despite the heavy weight pushing at her eyelids, trying to draw her back under.

Her eyes creaked open, but her surroundings were too dark to see anything. She only knew that she wasn't anyplace familiar. Her heart pounded in her chest at the startling realization. She remembered getting home. She put down her purse and keys and turned to shut the door.

She could almost picture a form in her doorway. A man smiling and reaching out to her. But the image was gone again before she could latch onto it.

She looked down, her eyes beginning to adjust to the dark. She was sitting in a chair, her wrists tied to the arms of it. No, not tied.

Taped. Duct taped.

A whimper escaped her throat at the realization that something very bad had happened. Something was very wrong and she wasn't safe. She wasn't okay.

Tiff's heart rate slammed into overdrive and the fog began to clear from her head. She needed to get out. She needed to run.

Her thoughts went to Ronan. God how she wished he was here. Would he come looking for her if he couldn't reach her?

She struggled against the bindings at her wrists, pushing past the weakness she felt in her limbs to try to loosen the tape. If she could loosen it, she might be able to slip her arms free and figure out where she was. Figure out how to get out of there.

Tiff froze, her skin breaking out with goose bumps at a scuffing noise from the corner. Someone was with her.

Heart beating too fast, she ran through the possibilities. Another prisoner? Her captor?

"Try to relax," came a voice from the same corner. A man's voice.

Tiff whimpered again, knowing what might happen to her. What this man who'd taken her might want.

"I only want to talk."

Anger shot through her, heightened and driven by her fear. "You should have come to my office hours!"

Silence.

Tiff waited, searching the dark, but it was no use. The corner she was facing was too dark, shrouded in shadows that protected the speaker from her view.

"Who's there?" she said, wanting him to speak again. Maybe if she could figure out who this was, she could talk him out of whatever this was. "What do you want?"

"The truth. I want to tell you the truth, so you can tell the world about it."

CHAPTER 21

EVERY MUSCLE IN RONAN'S BODY FELT LOCKED INTO PLACE AS he stood rigid in Tiff's apartment. There was nothing to indicate she'd been harmed or kidnapped or anything, other than the left-behind purse and phone.

Her car stood in her assigned spot out front. The apartment was quiet and orderly, as if she'd simply stepped away and hadn't returned.

Zach was on the phone with the captain trying to explain why they needed crime scene technicians at the apartment of a woman who had consulted with them on the case when there wasn't much to point to a problem.

Shauna reentered the apartment. "No answer from most of the neighbors. A retired man who lives three doors up said he saw her come home two hours ago when he was coming home from a walk. He doesn't remember seeing anyone or anything in the parking lot or near her apartment. He didn't hear anything."

Ronan clenched his hands into fists, focusing on his breathing. He wanted to punch something. He wanted to grab the phone from his partner and scream at the captain until he sent out a crime scene unit. He wanted something to fight. Someone to beat to a pulp until they brought Tiff back, safe. Alive.

He released his fists, stretching his fingers out, trying to shake off the feeling. His eyes met Shauna's.

She had been through this. She'd been taken and drugged, but they found her.

"If something's happened to her," Shauna said, "we'll get her back. Tiff's smart. She'll stay calm and when she gets the chance, she'll fight back."

Ronan's voice sounded strangled when he spoke; the pressure had a hold on his throat muscles as well. "Does she know how?"

They'd never talked about it. In fact, they hadn't talked about much. Two dates, really. Or half dates. But he'd never felt this kind of pull to another woman before. He'd wanted so much more with her, and the thought that she might be hurt or scared gutted him.

Shauna nodded. "She does. She's been to self-defense classes. She knows what she's doing. She'll keep her head and look for openings."

Zach got off the phone, stepping closer to them and putting a hand on Shauna's back. No doubt he was remembering when he'd been through this with Shauna.

"The captain is sending out a team. They'll check for prints and see if there's anything we can't see with the naked eye."

Ronan knew what that meant. Blood spatter.

But there wouldn't have been time to clean up, would there? If she was here two hours ago, no way someone could grab her and clean up a mess like that.

Ronan shoved the thought away and focused on what he could do. "If we assume this is linked to her consulting for us on this case, we need to track this killer now. We're out of time."

Zach and Shauna looked grim as they nodded. There were too many things they didn't know. No idea who the killer was or what the link was to the Howell kids. No idea why someone would want to hurt Tiff because of the case. No idea, even, if this was related to their case or something completely different. They could be chasing ghosts and shadows while Tiff fought for her life.

CHAPTER 22

R ONAN'S THUMB BEAT A STEADY RHYTHM ON HIS DESK AS HE closed his eyes and tried to figure out what they were missing.

He and Zach had returned to the precinct, despite the fact every ounce of his being screamed at Ronan to get out and hunt for Tiff.

Shauna had gone to the state cold case division to see if she could track down anything in the Howell case they'd missed. If she could pull the old files from storage, they might have some small fact that could help.

He tuned out the sounds around him, shoving aside for the moment the fact that the forensics techs hadn't found anything in her apartment. No footprints or blood trace evidence. No hairs that didn't belong to Tiff. No fingerprints on the doorknob. The only compelling thing they had found was the fact that there were *no* fingerprints on the knob. Not Tiff's or anyone else's.

The doorknob had been wiped clean, telling Ronan he was right when his gut screamed at him that something had happened to Tiff.

The captain agreed and now had officers looking for her and more canvassing the apartment complex to see if anyone had seen anything.

Surely no one could grab her and walk out of her apartment without anyone seeing anything?

Except they could. The building was mostly rented by people who worked during the day. Although the hallways and entrances were well lit, there were no cameras installed that might show them what happened.

Ronan's mind flipped through the case, from day one. He ran through the information a piece at a time. Ran through the day Tiff had put the pieces of the case together for them. Ran through everything she'd told them about the Howell children and the murders that started this all.

Ronan's thumb stilled, but he kept his eyes closed. There was something there. Something lurking in his mind. Like a piece of the puzzle that had been pressed into a spot it didn't belong in, just to try to make it work.

He opened his eyes. Teddy Howell.

Tiff had known so much about the Howell case. Every detail that was available to find. From the younger siblings, to who testified, and who represented whom.

How could she have missed the fact that Teddy Howell was dead? Tiff was much too passionate about getting history right, particularly dark history that might have lessons to teach. Teddy Howell's death wasn't something she would have overlooked.

And it hadn't turned up in their follow-up either.

"What?" Zach asked, meeting Ronan's gaze.

"Tiff didn't know Teddy Howell was dead."

Zach frowned. "So she missed it. Or forgot about it. It's been years since she researched the case."

Ronan shook his head. "She went back and checked her notes. She wouldn't have missed that fact."

Zach raised an eyebrow. "Are you saying you don't believe Dr. Taylor?"

Ronan shook his head, letting his eyes go fuzzy as he let the thought form in his head. There was an idea here. He only needed to give it the space to take shape.

He thought back to their interview with Sheila Taylor. Had there been anything strange about her? Had there been any signs that she was lying?

Curious, he pulled up a browser on his computer to search Dr. Sheila Taylor, wanting to look a little closer into her credentials, and any possible mentioning of her in the news.

They hadn't looked into her much since they'd been in such a hurry to protect her.

"Damnit!" Ronan smacked his desk with the heel of his hand. "Fuck!"

The department froze around him, all eyes turned his way, but it was Zach who spoke. "What?"

Captain Calhoun stepped out of his office, probably to fine Ronan for his swearing, but instead he moved to stand beside Ronan's desk. Maybe he knew Ronan was close to losing control. Maybe he was willing to give him a break this once. Ronan didn't care.

All he cared about was what he'd just found.

Ronan moved his monitor so Zach and the captain could see the picture of Dr. Sheila Taylor. They'd been in such a hurry to protect the woman, they hadn't done more than grab her address before hitting the road.

On his computer screen, an Asian woman who was by no means the woman they had interviewed the day before looked out at them.

Ronan looked at his captain. "I don't know what's going on here, but the woman Hartford PD has a protective detail on is not Dr. Sheila Taylor."

CHAPTER 23

IF THEIR FUCKUP WAS THE REASON TIFF GOT HURT, RONAN wouldn't forgive himself. It was scary how strongly he felt about her and the lengths to which he would go to punish whomever had taken her. None of that mattered now. What mattered was that he fix this.

"We need to confirm every detail," Ronan said, as Zach called Hartford to have the officers take their imposter into custody and go to the doctor's house to see if she was alive, though Ronan doubted she was.

The other detectives gathered around as Ronan went to the board and pointed at the pictures. "I want someone on each of these people, confirming who they are, and where and when they died. Check everything."

He looked at the image of Addie Howell, taking in her stringy brown hair, thin lips, high cheeks, and blue eyes.

The psychiatrist they'd spoken to had a gaunt face and graying hair. But she'd also had thin lips and big, prominent blue eyes.

He looked to the image of Addie Howell's mother. She shared the same eyes as her daughter.

Those eyes were virtually impossible to mistake, but they'd looked right into them and hadn't made the link. Why would they? He recalled the surprise on their imposter's face when they asked about the Howell case—the haunted look she'd worn when discussing Addie and Teddy.

She'd seemed nothing but genuine.

Zach and the captain came up behind him as the other detectives hurried to double- and triple-check everything they knew.

Zach took a black marker and sketched the short dark bob from the fake Dr. Taylor onto the picture of Addie's mother.

"We couldn't have talked to a ghost," Zach said. "And Mrs. Howell is most definitely dead."

"No," Ronan said, capping the pen and tossing it onto a nearby table. "But we might have found Mrs. Howell's estranged sister."

He turned and looked at them. "Think about it. We've been thinking the younger siblings were behind this, but the woman we met was too old to be the younger Howell girl. We know for a fact Addie's mother was murdered since half the trial was about her death. There's no one else it could be."

"And she might be very angry at the treatment her niece and nephew received," Zach said, his face grim. "She might see what happened as an injustice when the children took matters into their own hands after no one would help the children escape their abuser."

Ronan went to his computer and pulled up articles from the time of the Howell murders, zeroing in on one of the Howell family. He zoomed in and studied the faces of each of the Howell kids and the mother and father, wanting to be sure they didn't make the same mistake again.

Zach was at his computer. "I'm tracking the sister." He tapped his keys.

Ronan took in the features of the Howell girls. The dark hair and bright blue eyes. The high cheekbones.

The resemblance was a little less evident with the boys. Ronan studied Teddy Howell. The thin lips were there, but his eyes were a grayish brown and his face fuller.

"Mrs. Howell's sister might have been estranged from the family, but she didn't go far. Nancy Renard lives in New Jersey where she works as a loan officer in a bank." Zach turned his monitor toward Ronan. "And she's definitely our fake doctor."

There was no mistaking her. Nancy Renard was in Connecticut. Was she their killer?

Ronan looked back to the image of Teddy Howell. "There's something about him."

"You think you've seen him before?" Captain Calhoun asked, no accusation in his voice, though that didn't matter.

At this point, Ronan was full of recrimination for himself and the way he'd fucked up on this case.

He scanned his memory, trying desperately to figure out why the stocky boy looked familiar. Hoping to jog his memory, he looked toward the murder board, letting his eyes roam over each name he had written on there.

And then he stopped at Ted Hadley, the contractor. The memory of him in the garage cleaning up came back—his burly figure in paint-stained pants with his tools strewn about the space. It had been too easy to believe he belonged there.

Hell, he probably had belonged there. Noah Barrett probably had hired him to do the shelves. It would have been all too easy for Ted Hadley to get work with him and use that as the perfect ruse to get Noah Barrett out of his house. Noah could have come into the garage to check Ted's progress. All it would take is a crack over the head with a wrench and Ted could have put Noah into his own car and backed it right up the drive with no one the wiser.

Ted Hadley had gray-brown eyes and thin lips...

Ted Hadley. Same initials as Teddy Howell...

In complete disbelief, Ronan turned to Zach, who was still studying the photo and trying to figure it out. "You know him too. Ted Hadley is Teddy Howell."

"Oh hell..." Zach stared at the screen in disbelief, but Ronan could tell that he too now recognized Ted Hadley in the photo.

All the while, Ronan's panic grew. The last time he'd spoken to Ted Hadley, he'd come to report seeing the black BMW parked outside of Noah Barrett's house. A shameless attempt to turn suspicion away from himself and pretend he was trying to help move along the investigation.

A chill swept over Ronan's body as he recalled the conversation he overheard Jepsen having with Ted when he and Zach had been on their way to check on the Barrott children.

It was an easy conversation to remember because they'd been talking about Tiff.

And now Tiff is missing... Fear unlike anything Ronan had ever felt before engulfed him. He sprang up from his seat. "JEPSEN!" he bellowed.

"Whoa, what's going on?" Zach asked, also rising from his seat, arms out to try to calm Ronan.

This was usually the other way around. Zach frequently had to count to twenty or take himself out of a room to calm down when his anger got the best of him.

Not Ronan. Ronan was the iceman. He might have emotions swirling through him, but he never showed them. He made sure he didn't react to things on the outside.

He'd been that way from the moment he figured out the trick worked on bullies. If you didn't let them see you sweat, they left you alone a lot faster.

But not now. Not with this. His emotions roiled and spilled over, swamping him.

His captain tried to step in the way, but Ronan moved around him, zeroing in on Jepsen.

He was so furious he was practically shaking as he grabbed Jepsen in the break room, the other man's half-eaten bagel falling to the floor.

The puzzle had finally come together in Ronan's mind, and he knew he needed to act fast.

Jepsen blinked, but then he opened his big fat mouth. The one he'd never learned to keep shut. "You need to get out more, Cafferty. Looks like the job is wearing on you."

Ronan shoved Jepsen up against the wall. "We told you to take down Ted Hadley's statement, but you started talking to him about Tiff Carson instead!"

Jepsen stared back at him, affronted. "What are you talking about? I did take down his statement."

"Did you or did you not talk to him about Tiffany Carson?" Ronan ground out, feeling Zach's arm on him, but shoving his partner back.

Jepsen's face darkened. "So what? So what if I did, you fucking psycho?"

"What did you tell him about her?" Ronan demanded, barely registering as the captain shoved himself between Jepsen and Ronan, forcing Ronan to back off.

"Whoa, back up, detective," Jepsen said warningly. "Let's

not get ourselves carried away here. What is this *really* about? You have a thing for Tiffany or something?" He narrowed his eyes and smirked. "I get it. She's a beautiful woman."

"Jepsen, I swear to God, if you don't tell me what you talked about, I'm going to beat the shit out..."

"Whoa... All right, all right," Zach said, forcibly placing himself between Ronan and Jepsen opposite the captain and using his body to shove his partner back. "Let's calm down." He gave Ronan a meaningful gaze. "Seriously, settle down, partner. This isn't going to get you anywhere."

"Did you just threaten me, Cafferty?" Jepsen said, shouted.

"He's under a lot of pressure right now," Zach said over his shoulder, still pushing against Ronan's chest.

The captain turned on Jepsen. "Stuff the attitude, Jep. I need to know right now what you told Ted Hadley. Tiff Carson is missing and it's possible he's behind it."

Jepsen frowned, his defiance replaced with what actually looked like concern. Ronan didn't care though. It was taking every ounce of strength not to go after him again.

He wanted to lash out. Wanted to make someone hurt.

Jepsen shook his head. "Honestly, Captain, I didn't say much. All I said was that she was going to find out the truth about the Herschel Kenworth case because she's good at what she does."

You sealed her fate, Ronan thought. If Ted Hadley was really one of the murderous Howell kids, the last thing Tiff needed was for him to think she was skilled enough to find out the truth regarding the Howells.

Did he think she might figure out who he was? Had Jepsen sold her skills that well?

It seemed unlikely, but he couldn't figure out what other reason someone would have for taking Tiff.

Ronan deflated. They might have some idea of who had Tiff, but they had no clue where to look for her.

CHAPTER 24

Shauna O'Rourke was with the team that went to Dr. Taylor's house after getting the call from Zach. She'd been completely flabbergasted to learn that the woman had been an imposter. In fact, as someone who prided herself on being good at her job, the woman's deception felt like a personal offense.

Right now, though, they needed to see if the real Dr. Taylor was still alive.

Shauna stood on the porch of the house they'd found the imposter in and pressed the doorbell, uniformed cops standing at her back.

She pounded on the door. "Dr. Taylor?" she called out. "Dr. Taylor, this is the Hartford Police Department! Please, open up."

Still no answer.

Trepidation running through her, Shauna glanced back at her accompanying cops and nodded, letting them step in front of her with a Halligan bar to pry open the door.

A minute later, they entered the house, weapons drawn and moving through the space to clear the house.

The first floor was empty and quiet. The only indication of someone being home was the kitchen light being on.

The dishes were clean, and there was a very faint smell of food in the air, as if a meal had not long ago been prepared.

Their imposter had been staying here, with units posted outside at all times to protect her. It was almost maddening.

She was already in custody and would face questioning soon.

A team of officers moved up the stairs while Shauna and two others moved through the kitchen to the first of two doors at the back of the room.

Shauna opened the first. The pantry, filled with stacked boxes of pasta and canned vegetables.

She shut the door and turned to the other one.

Shauna pulled the door open as the other officers covered her, revealing a descending staircase.

The basement, she thought.

She descended the stairs, her weapon balanced above her flashlight to allow her to see into the dark, the officers following closely behind her.

Halfway down, one of the steps creaked. Shauna and the officers froze, allowing several seconds to pass. When nothing happened, they resumed.

The scent of decay hit Shauna's nose. She inwardly groaned, knowing precisely what they were about to walk into.

The real Dr. Taylor was sprawled on the floor, lying in a pool of blood, a jagged slash in her throat. Her face and arms were bruised.

Shauna sighed and bowed her head, while the cops accompanying her proceeded to search the basement.

Shauna already knew they wouldn't find anyone. This killer had been one step ahead of law enforcement for a long time.

She pulled out her phone and called Zach. "Sheila Taylor is dead. I'm looking at her right now. She's been beaten and had her throat slashed right here in her own basement."

"Dammit," Zach muttered.

"Tell me about it," Shauna said.

Zach filled her in on what they knew about Nancy and Teddy Howell.

"I'll go sit in on the interrogation of Nancy Renard. The officers on her protective detail scooped her up and are headed in with her now."

CHAPTER 25

Z ACH POUNDED ON THE DOOR OF T ED H ADLEY'S RENTED house to no avail as Ronan scanned the premises.

Cal and Jarrod had come with them, each of them fully aware how hard it was to know someone you cared about was in danger like this. They'd been there themselves and would know every breath Ronan took was an effort against the crushing pressure on his chest.

Cal and Jarrod circled around to the back of the house. All the doors seemed locked and secured, and there was no vehicle nearby.

Ronan hadn't expected to find him here, but his blood still boiled as he stared up at the locked house. They needed to get in and see if they could find anything to tell them where he might have gone with Tiff.

Cal came around the side of the house, relaying the news that Captain Calhoun had obtained a warrant to enter the premises.

Ronan didn't need to be told twice. He bolted up the stairs, raising a booted foot to kick at the door near its lock. It opened with a satisfying crack of wood.

The house was two floors but they cleared it with a regimented efficiency. It was empty.

The upstairs was significantly smaller than the downstairs area, sporting a bathroom, a short hallway, a linen closet, and two bedrooms. Intuition guiding him, Ronan entered the main bedroom.

He dug through the man's life, using his flashlight to look under the bed. He searched the closet, and then the dressers, pushing aside piles of clothes. He pushed back curtains, checking windowsills. He searched the drawers of the nightstand. He looked behind the television.

Nothing, nothing, and more nothing.

Not willing to give up though, he moved into the bathroom, giving pause at a tube of lipstick on the bathroom counter, next to the hand soap.

Did that confirm that he and his aunt were in touch? They had to be, right?

He pulled back the shower curtain, finding shampoo and a bar of soap.

He turned around and opened the bathroom cabinet. Toothpaste, deodorant, and bottles of sleeping pills.

"Shit," he said, slamming the bathroom cabinet back shut.

He moved to the second bedroom where Jarrod was, but the room looked bare. A dresser and bed.

Still, Jarrod had opened the dresser drawers and was now shifting it to look behind. Ronan turned to check in with the rest of the team to see what they'd found when he saw a folder shoved between the wall and the bed. He knelt and tugged at the corner, losing a few of the papers to the space under the bed as he pulled it out.

It didn't matter. What he saw was enough.

Jarrod joined him and they fished through articles and

pictures about Noah Barrett. Some printed from the internet, but others were pictures someone had taken of Noah outside his home. Noah walking up the steps to his church. Noah's car, office building. All of it.

There were pictures of Noah's father, Luis Barrett, though fewer of those as if Ted hadn't had to stalk him long before he had the opportunity to take him.

Ronan moved to the bed and fished out the papers that had fallen underneath it. He flipped them over and pain raked through him, followed by a cold, hard determination.

Ted Hadley had been following Tiff. At her work. Outside her apartment. Sitting in a coffee shop.

He'd been following her and now he had her.

CHAPTER 26

RONAN HIT THE STAIRS WITH JARROD BEHIND HIM, SHOUTING for Zach as he ran for the first floor.

Zach didn't question him when Ronan headed for the door, only following and calling to Jarrod and Cal to secure the scene.

"He was stalking Tiff," Ronan said. "He's got her." Ronan's blood boiled. How had this guy fooled them all so well?

Zach was dialing Shauna as Ronan drove, heading north toward Hartford. They had Ted's aunt. She had to know where he would take Tiff.

It was impossible not to picture Tiff taking the kind of beating Ted had doled out to his other victims. Rancid dread pooled in Ronan's stomach at the thought of her suffering that kind of abuse and pain.

If Ted was killing her because he feared she would dig up the truth about the murders, would he skip the torture? He had no need for vengeance from her.

But that might mean she was dead already and that thought was more than Ronan could handle.

Pray she's being tortured so there's a chance to save her?

Zach cut the call with Shauna, and Ronan realized he hadn't heard any of it.

"Did she get anything yet?"

"No," Zach said. "Shauna had the Hartford Police Department bring her to the cold case division at the state criminal division in Rocky Hill, but she's refusing to talk. She asked for a lawyer and they're waiting for one from the public defender's office."

With sirens screaming and lights flashing, they reached Rocky Hill, Connecticut, in ten minutes.

Ronan stood beside Shauna and Zach, watching Nancy Renard through the observation window of the interrogation room. It was taking everything he had not to run into that room and demand to know where Ted had Tiff.

"How much longer?" he ground out through clenched teeth.

Shauna turned to face him, hands on hips. "It won't matter how much longer if you can't get control of yourself. My boss isn't going to let you so much as sit in on the interrogation, much less lead it with you looking like this. Bring out the iceman routine."

Ronan fisted his hands in his hair and pulled. She was right. He'd lost control and if he didn't get his shit together, Tiff was going to pay the price.

He moved to the corner of the small room and put his hands on his knees, bent double. As he stared at the floor, he focused on his breathing. And he let all of it go. The panic and fear of not knowing where Tiff was. The anger that she'd been taken by a madman. The guilt that this happened to her because of him.

Steady breath in. Steady breath out.

He pushed it all out of his mind and shut down his emotions. He'd done it before. He would do it again.

When Shauna let him know ten minutes later that a lawyer had arrived and was in with Nancy Renard, Ronan was ready.

He turned and faced Shauna's boss, Supervisory Assistant State's Attorney Vivian Cullis, head of the state's cold case unit. She was a tall woman in her late fifties with steely black eyes and short black hair.

He didn't wait for her to say anything before he made his pitch. "I'd like to take the lead on questioning. This involves a cold case, but that's in Massachusetts not Connecticut. We respect and appreciate the help you've provided on the case, but we have an active case and a missing consultant who's in grave danger."

She raised her brows.

Ronan added a "ma'am" for good measure.

Cullis leaned sideways to look around Ronan at Shauna.

Shauna's eyes were on Ronan when she nodded. "He makes some very valid points. I'm comfortable with Detective Cafferty taking the lead."

Cullis looked at Ronan. "Very well, detective, but remember you're in my house. Don't break the rules and don't muck it up or I'll have your head."

Ronan nodded and, when she stepped to the side, he moved around her with his partner at his back.

They entered the room to see Nancy and a short black woman with round cheeks and sharp eyes sitting side by side at the table. They stopped whispering and looked up when the detectives entered.

"You ready for us?" Ronan asked, all politeness and deference. He knew exactly where he was going with this.

The attorney eyed him with the kind of look that said she was onto his bullshit but she nodded.

Ronan opened the folder Shauna's team had prepared for him while they waited for the attorney and sat across the table from the pair. After taking care of logistical issues like acknowledgement of the video and audio recordings taking place and a rereading of Ms. Renard's rights, he pulled the full-color photos of each of the victims from both Massachusetts and Connecticut out of the folder and spread them on the desk.

He stabbed a finger on each of the Massachusetts victims. "Massachusetts."

He did the same with the Connecticut ones. "Connecticut."

Renard's blue eyes avoided the images, focusing on him with wide eyes that told him she was frightened.

Good. She should be.

"You and Teddy crossed state lines. We'll be asking the federal government to bring federal charges." He would let her lawyer explain to her that no one wanted to be in federal court where sentences were often much harsher than a state court.

The lawyer shook her head. "You can't argue single course of conduct for murders that took place years apart."

Ronan didn't even look her way. "Be my guest. Roll the dice on that one."

Renard shook her head, still refusing to look at the pictures. "I didn't have anything to do with the murders. That wasn't me."

Ronan grinned and leaned closer. "Doesn't matter. You lied to police officers. You impeded an investigation. For nearly a day, you continued that ruse while officers provided a security detail to you thinking you were Teddy's next victim."

He pushed the picture of Dr. Sheila Taylor's brutalized body toward her. "You cooked dinner in Sheila Taylor's house while her body lay dead in the basement. You slept in her bed and went to her office the next day where you cancelled all her appointments for the day so you wouldn't get caught. You can argue all you want that you weren't part of these murders, but I think a jury is going to see that differently."

Her face was ashen by the time he was finished and her voice was small when she said, "I didn't sleep in her bed."

Her lawyer put a hand on Renard's arm, but it was too late. Renard had started talking.

Ronan shook his head, letting out a bitter laugh and nearly losing his hold on his emotions. He shoved them down, though. He could do this. "You were getting out of the shower when our team arrived. Do you think our medical examiner is going to tell us Sheila Taylor's body was still warm in the basement when that happened? When you put on her clothes and pretended to be her?"

Large tears began a slow trek down Renard's face but she didn't speak.

He moved to what really mattered and what he hoped would get her talking. He was banking on his ability to read her. Banking on the fact that he really didn't think she was a coldhearted killer.

He removed the last photo from the folder, this one a shot of Tiff they'd taken from Shauna's phone. It showed Tiff smiling at the camera, her hair blowing in the wind as she sat under an umbrella on a beach. She was relaxed and laughing with friends on a girls' weekend at the shore.

He laid it on top of the ugly crime scene photos, letting

the dichotomy stand out. He pointed at it. "This is Tiffany Carson. She's a professor and an author. She's a daughter and a sister."

He wanted to say, "She's a girlfriend, *my* girlfriend," but it wasn't strictly true after only two almost dates, and it wouldn't help here. He went on instead. "She's not related to the Howells or Addie and Teddy's case. She was consulting for us, that's all."

Nancy Renard's eyes dropped to the photo of Tiff and stayed locked there. He had her.

He pointed at Tiff's smiling face. "Teddy has her. We don't know what he's planning but with what he's done to his other victims, this doesn't look good. Do yourself a favor and show that you aren't like him. That you want to put an end to this and you're willing to help."

He waited as her tears flowed freely and then carefully, saying each word slowly, he spoke. "Help us save her."

Her attorney looked at him. "Give us a moment please, detectives."

Ronan didn't want to. He wanted to scream and rail and get his answers. But he nodded and stood, leaving behind the photos as he and Zach exited the room.

Several minutes later, they returned to the room where Nancy Renard agreed to tell them everything in exchange for a recommendation for leniency from Shauna's boss.

Ronan sat rigid as Renard spoke.

"Teddy found me six years ago. Renard isn't my maiden name. I was remarried twice over the years and I didn't know he was looking for me, so..." She let the thought fall with a shrug. "My childhood wasn't a good one and by the time I got away from my family, I wanted nothing to do with any of them. Not even my little sister, Teddy's mom."

She traced her fingers over the now-empty table in front

of her. "We were physically and emotionally abused by our parents, but I got the brunt of it because I was different." Now she looked up. "I was never right according to them. My parents were the kind of Christians who twisted everything about what is right in religion to use it to harm. Having a gay daughter was unacceptable.

"In their minds, they could beat it out of me. My sister got some of the abuse, but she was a good girl. She stayed in line and if she did catch a beating from Dad, she fully believed it was her fault and she needed to reflect on her behavior so it wouldn't happen again."

"Did you see the news coverage about the kids? When Teddy and Addie killed their parents?" Zach asked.

"Not for several years. At the time I was living in a commune in Ohio. I'd gone from an abusive family to what I now know was essentially a cult and we didn't have much to do with the outside world. Twelve years later, I reemerged and eventually read an account of the crimes."

"Did you try to find the other kids? Or reach out to Teddy?" Ronan asked.

"No." She leveled them with a look. "I wasn't any use to those kids. It wasn't for another ten years or more that I was able to hold down a good job and have even semihealthy relationships."

Ronan needed to move her forward. They needed to know about Teddy and where he would have taken Tiff. "So Teddy found you. What then?"

"I was back in Massachusetts then. My parents were dead and there was no reason not to go back at that point. My second wife and I lived there for three years before she died and I was alone. Teddy tracked me down somehow and we began to get to know each other. He did house repair and carpentry so he moved closer to where I was so we could be a bit of a support system to each other."

Ronan kept his face neutral. She'd supported him through his murder spree.

"He wanted to look for his younger siblings but I convinced him it was better to let them be. They probably had good lives. So, he and I saw each other every week or so for dinner and he did his thing."

"Until the first murder four years ago?" Ronan asked. "Gretchen Meyer."

She nodded. "He was working on her house and he recognized her. She was the social worker who'd been assigned to their case when Addie tried to tell someone about the abuse. She didn't recognize him, of course. He was a grown man, but she hadn't seen him since he was fourteen. I think that more than anything sent him into a rage."

She met Ronan's eyes and firmed her expression. "I didn't know about that one until later. I swear."

Convenient. Ronan nodded, keeping his thoughts to himself.

"It sparked something within him. He started looking for the others involved in the case."

"Who did he go after next?" Zach asked.

"The prosecutor." She shook her head. "I didn't make the connection when it was the social worker even though I saw the news of her death. I didn't recognize her name. But when I saw the name of the prosecutor it jogged something.

Still, I didn't want to believe he could be capable of that and so I didn't ask. I convinced myself he couldn't be responsible for the man's death. Years later though, he suddenly wanted to move to New Haven. I knew it had to be for a reason, so I started doing some research, trying to figure out who he was after this time. I found his notes about Noah Barrett, the kid next door who implied that Addie and

Teddy were..." She swallowed. "That they weren't *decent* brother and sister. Teddy hated him for that, and so far as I know there was never any truth to them. It was just one more jab at two kids who had endured hell together."

"So you moved to New Haven?" Ronan asked.

"No. I refused to come. I confronted him and he admitted what he'd done. I tried to stop him but he was too angry. Teddy came here and for a long time I didn't see anything in the news. I thought maybe he changed his mind even though he wasn't taking my calls anymore."

"Teddy bided his time for six months looking for his next victim, but you thought he'd just give up?" Zach asked, disbelief in his voice at the way this woman buried her head in the sand. Ronan understood the sentiment.

She didn't answer the accusation, simply continuing with her story. "Eventually I came down here to find him. He had already worked his way into the community. Working at the church, making friends with the parishioners. Doing work for them. And then, finally, Noah hired him for some work around his house.

"I tried to stop him and he told me he only wanted to talk to him."

Ronan held very still, knowing if he let himself say what he wanted to, he could ruin this and she'd stop talking.

"I hoped to convince him what he was doing wasn't right, even though I understood why he was doing it. But he managed to leave the house without me noticing. He hasn't been back home since then. I think that was when he killed Noah. I did my own research and found everyone else connected with the case. I caught up with him at Sheila Taylor's house but I was too late."

"What happened?" Zach said.

She swallowed. "I walked in on him right as he killed

her." A tear fell from her eye and she looked down at her chest. "The blood sprayed me." She buried her head in her hands. "I'm sorry. I showered off the blood and when the police showed up at the door, I covered for him. I couldn't admit the truth of what he'd done."

"All right. I get that you were trying to protect your nephew," Zach began calmly.

"But you need to make this right," Ronan interrupted, an edge entering his voice. "How do we find him, Ms. Renard? Where would he take Tiff?"

CHAPTER 27

As Tiff's eyes adjusted to the gloom around her, she searched the room—a large and spacious area. A warehouse and, from the looks of it, the place hadn't been used in ages. It was empty and dusty.

The man had left her there after his cryptic message that he wanted her to tell the truth. Her mouth was dry and her head pounded, but she knew she needed to assess her situation and find a way out of it.

She was supposed to meet Shauna for lunch, so hopefully her friend would figure out something was wrong. And if not Shauna, then Ronan? They'd been talking regularly. Would he realize he hadn't heard from her or would he assume she was busy with work or had lost interest in him?

She'd give anything right now to be with him. To be out of this nightmare and in his arms, surrounded by that confident strength and his calm, steady way.

She rocked her hands back and forth within the tape, not caring that it hurt. The tape was loosening. If she could get her hands loose, she could free her feet and run.

If not out the door, then she'd get out some other way.

There were windows in the space. Only a few and most were boarded over. She'd have to climb to get to them but she would find a way.

As she kept up her efforts, she searched the room for anything she could use as a weapon. There were piles of debris in some of the corners. Should she search there if she got loose so she had some way of fighting back or should she just try to escape?

The door opened at the far end of the space, letting in a shaft of light that hit her eyes and made her wince. She shut her eyes against the light but knew she needed to open them.

She couldn't hide from what was happening. She squinted against the light and watched the figure as he stepped into the room.

He came toward her, holding out a water bottle. "You're probably thirsty," he said, opening the cap. She heard the crack of the seal. Could he have tampered with the water in some other way? With a needle or something?

Would he go to those lengths? She was sure she'd been drugged when he took her. It was the only thing that would account for her grogginess and the emptiness where memory should be.

He tilted the water at her lips for her and she sipped, praying there was nothing in it.

The cold water soothed her throat and she swallowed greedily, wondering how long she'd been in the chair. Her body ached from the stillness, and she prayed he didn't notice that the tape at her wrists was loose.

When he lowered the bottle, he stepped back and she looked at him, studying his face.

Maybe she shouldn't. Maybe she should have tried to

convince him she hadn't seen his face so she had a better shot of convincing him to let her go.

Too late.

As she looked, though, realization dawned and she knew who she was looking at. The man who'd audited her class. He'd sat in her classroom listening to her lecture.

He'd stepped in and given her an out when James was pressuring her on campus. That nice man. She shuddered at the realization.

But there was more. How had she missed it before?

She'd looked at pictures of this man as a boy. And she'd looked at pictures of his father.

She was looking at a grown-up Teddy Howell.

Tiff remained perfectly quiet. Why did he think she could do something for him? Tell the world the truth, he'd said.

"I brought you here to tell you a story," Teddy began. "And I want you to pay attention to every word. I want you to know firsthand what it was like growing up with Larry Howell as a father...

"It's almost impossible to fully express the horrors he forced onto my older sister, Addie. He was a monster."

Tiff watched Teddy and the pain on his face. It was astonishing, the way he seemed teleported back in time, as if the events he recalled had happened just yesterday.

"Our mother was no better. She knew what was happening but she told Addie to keep her mouth shut and do as she was told." His mouth twisted. "Addie tried to leave once and Mom caught her. She beat her with a belt, all the while telling Addie it was for her own good.

"She'd say Addie needed to learn to behave."

He grimaced and stared Tiff in the eyes. "Do you have any

idea how it felt for me to witness how helpless and ashamed that man made Addie feel every night? What kind of man rapes his own daughter? And what kind of mother lets it happen?"

Tiff couldn't speak.

"Mothers are supposed to love and protect their children." His words held the plea of a child, desperate for a parent who loved him.

Teddy swallowed, his eyes glistening. "Addie would beg him to stop... She would cry and tell him he was hurting her, but he didn't care." He looked at her, pleading in his eyes. "He was never going to stop."

Tiff's stomach churned, listening to such an awful story.

"I was too afraid to go into Addie's room to help her fight him off. So instead, I would go into either Ashley's or Johnny's room, hugging them and rocking them to sleep, to sing them lullabies so they wouldn't overhear the horror happening down the hall.

Teddy stopped and looked past Tiff, his eyes haunted as though he was still that little boy. "Until one night, he came to Ashley's room instead..."

Tiff shuddered, sorrow gutting her for these children and what they'd been through even though his actions as an adult horrified her.

He looked back at her. "No one was going to stop it. No one helped. Not the social worker, not the teacher Addie told. They believed our parents because everyone saw them as perfect."

So many adults had failed them. They hadn't had anyone they could count on.

If this happened now, would people see their actions as self-defense or would it all end as horribly as it had forty years ago?

What would she have done in the Howell children's shoes?

It was a question she didn't like contemplating.

He bent and came forward, leaning to see Tiff better. "Don't you see? The horror didn't stop after my parents were dead. Because that's when the social workers and psychiatrist and judges and every-damned-body else who didn't help us suddenly wanted to step forward and determine our fate. Not a single one of them considered what we'd been through."

His anger was clearly growing as he spoke, and Tiff tried to shrink back in the chair. Would he lash out at her? She whimpered, knowing what he'd done to his other victims.

His face grew red as he screamed at her. "They ignored the sick and twisted things going on in those bedrooms at night. They *blamed* us! Put us in jail."

He stopped suddenly, his face only inches from Tiff's. She couldn't breathe. Couldn't move.

His breath came in pants and she held his eyes, praying.

When she spoke, her voice shook and it only came out as a whisper. "What happened to you and your sister was wrong. So wrong, Teddy."

"Ted!" he bellowed.

Tiff jerked, shrinking in on herself.

He stood and paced away from her. "Ted. Ted Hadley. Teddy Howell was weak. A child who couldn't protect anyone. I stopped being that kid when Addie and I fought back and I won't ever go back to being that *victim*."

He spat out the word and Tiff knew she didn't want to be a victim either. She would be a survivor. She would make it through this.

Ted turned abruptly and walked to the door, shutting it behind him.

Tiff sat still, ears straining to hear him. Had he locked it? Was he gone?

Tiff began to count, holding herself very still.

She passed one hundred and kept going. One fifty. Two hundred. Four hundred.

When she thought she'd waited long enough, she began moving her wrists again, carefully, slowly, in case he came back. She would not be a victim.

CHAPTER 28

RONAN FELT THE TENSION IN HIS BODY BUILD AGAIN AS HE watched Nancy Renard. If Ted's aunt didn't know where he was, they'd have nothing to go on and the clock was ticking. Tiff had been missing for over six hours now.

God knows what she'd been through in those hours.

The officers and crime scene technicians at Ted's house had scoured it top to bottom for any hints at where he might have taken Tiff. There was nothing. Ted might have kept a file on his victims, but he didn't keep anything on the locations he took them to.

Ronan and Zach had detectives looking for any connection he might have had to the locations he used. Initially, they'd thought his work as a contractor must have been the connection to the buildings, but that had been a dead end.

Finally, Renard let out her breath with a whoosh and spoke. "When I first got to town, I didn't confront Ted right away. I watched him and followed him. I saw him drive by that building he took Noah to, and a few other places."

Ronan slid a pad and pencil in front of her and jabbed

the paper. "Write them all down. As much as you remember about where they were."

As he watched, she listed four spots in addition to the building where they'd found Noah.

Ronan took the page from her and mentally crossed off the building where they'd found Noah's father. That left three locations. He stood and left the room with the list, Zach behind him.

Shauna and her boss fell into step beside them as they moved down the hall.

"Nicely done, detective."

Ronan gave a nod in response to Cullis as they moved, but he was scanning the other three addresses on their list. They would need to send teams to each location, but he wanted to figure out which one was their best bet at finding Tiff. He'd be on the team going there.

"What have we got?" asked Hutch, one of the other detectives on Shauna's team, as he looked up from a laptop he'd set up at a large table in the cold case division's bullpen.

Ronan handed him the list and watched as Hutch began to enter the information into the laptop. The display on a nearby screen lit up and they were all able to see what Hutch was doing.

Other detectives from the cold case team gathered around, all of them ready to lend a hand. These guys were some of the best detectives out there and Ronan was grateful for their willingness to help.

Hutch pulled up maps of the areas where each budling was, moving them on the screen so all three were showing.

Ronan pointed to the one on the right. "This one is closest to her apartment."

"But it's also in the highest traffic area of all of them," Zach offered. "Would he have enough privacy there?"

Ronan flinched. They all knew Ted liked privacy for was his victims. He couldn't use a place where someone would hear the screams.

Detective Manigault, or Manny, stepped up and pointed to the area depicted in the map on the left. "I know this area. My aunt used to rent a warehouse for her business out there, but they were old. A storm took out a lot of the roofs and one of the places had bad wiring that led to a fire. So far as I know, all the businesses have relocated. It's isolated."

Hutch clicked on the corner of the map in the center to close it, saying, "This one's been demolished. Torn down two days ago."

Good. The spot Manny had pointed to was closer to where they were in Rocky Hill than it was to New Haven.

Ronan looked to Cullis. "Can your team back us up if we head to the most likely location? We can have our captain send units to the other one, just in case."

She gave a nod to her people. "Head out. Cafferty and Reynolds are taking point on this."

In minutes, they were rolling, headed toward what Ronan prayed was Tiff's rescue.

"We'll get her back," Zach said quietly from the passenger seat. "We'll bring her home."

CHAPTER 29

TIFF'S HANDS AND WRISTS WERE SWEATING NOW, HELPING WITH the tape. She'd stretched her bindings and now began twisting her wrists and pulling, working her wrists loose. Once her hands were loose, she had a shot at getting out of this.

Come on, come on... Tiff's heart pounded as she worked her wrists and watched the door.

One more wrench and she was free. She could almost hear her heart as it picked up its pace. Could feel it crash against her rib cage.

Yes! Her right hand came free. She flexed her fingers and shook out her arm before reaching to get the rest of the tape off her left hand.

Then she froze. The sound of keys in the front door stopped her cold. She couldn't get herself free fast enough to get out before he came in.

Tiff tried to shove her right hand back under the tape, but it was too late. Instead, she mashed her arm down over the tape and braced her arms in place as though she were still secured to the chair.

She needed more time. If he didn't notice her arms in the near-dark of the warehouse, she could try again the next time he left her alone.

If there was a next time.

Tiff held still and watched as Ted moved toward her.

He stopped eight feet away and looked at her.

"I'm sorry. I had to leave before my temper got the best of me."

"Okay," Tiff said, not sure how to talk to him. "I'm glad you did. What happened to you and Addie wasn't fair. I think you're right that the world needs to know your side of it. I can help you do that if you want to tell me about that night."

He looked into her eyes, his gaze blazing with intensity. "You promise you're going to tell my story? Addie's story?"

Tiff nodded. "Yes. It's an important story to tell."

She believed that. Stories like theirs were all too common. Not the way they'd killed their parents, but in the way the system had let them down. Too many children's voices went unheard. Too many went without help as they faced abuse and neglect.

"And you're going to tell it the right way?"

"Yes, Ted. I will."

Tiff's breath hitched in her throat, her nerves skyrocketing.

He nodded a few times, like he was trying to convince himself she'd told him the truth.

"Tell me what happened when your dad came to Ashley's room instead of Addie's. Were you in her room with her?"

Ted nodded again, this time slowly as his eyes got that glazed-over look again like he was looking between two worlds. Two times. He was here with Tiff but also back in his sister's bedroom forty years ago.

"I stood up to my father. I stood between him and Ashley's bed. I told him he couldn't touch her."

Tiff's chest tightened for those kids and the fear they must have felt. There was no way a boy as young as Ted had been then could have held his ground against his father.

"That must have taken incredible courage, Ted."

He looked at her and shook his head. "It wasn't enough. It didn't work. He backhanded me. It wasn't even much of a swing but I went flying. And then he locked me in her closet, and I had to listen while..."

Ted took a deep, shuddering breath and for a long time he didn't speak.

He looked so much smaller now as he relived the memory. "When it was over, Ashley let me out of the closet and I held her while she cried. Addie woke up and heard us. She realized what had happened.

"She and I put Ashley back to bed and told her it would be alright. We waited, sitting with her as she fell asleep." He stopped, looking as though he was still sitting at his sister's bed, waiting for her to go to sleep. Like he was trapped in that awful moment.

When he spoke again, he looked right at Tiff. "When she fell asleep, we snuck down to the garage. Dad didn't let us near his workshop, but Addie used an old brick to break open the padlock on his tool chest."

Tiff knew the details of the case. They used a hammer. Still, she waited, letting him speak. This part she was used to: letting survivors speak about their trauma in their own way and in their own time.

"Addie took his hammer and I took his hunting knife. Mom was drunk so she didn't even move when Addie hit our father in the head that first time. We knew we had to hit him hard and fast the first time so he didn't wake up. If he woke up, he would have killed us."

Ted's voice had become almost monotone now. Tiff had seen this, too. When someone wanted to get the telling over with. When they wanted it done so they wouldn't have to speak it any longer, they often went into a robotic retelling.

"She hit him eight times."

Tiff knew that from her research. His skull had been crushed on one side, his face nearly unrecognizable.

"And then I killed our mom. I used the knife and I ended it."

Despite her horror at what this man had done and the terror of not knowing what he was going to do to her, Tiff's heart ached for that little boy.

"I'm so sorry, Ted. I'm so sorry that happened to all of you." She reached toward him with her hand, wanting to comfort him. If she was doing this interview in her office or a survivor's home, she would offer him tissues and maybe sit by his side. It was never enough, but she always tried to be a comfort.

Tiff froze, realizing what she'd done, but it was too late.

Ted's eyes were focused on her free hand. Hot rage flared in them, replacing the anguish that had been there only moments before.

"I—" Tiff didn't get any further.

Ted's fist struck out and he hit her in the face, the force of it throwing the whole chair back. Pain sliced through her cheek and eye, bringing tears, as the back of her head hit the hard floor.

"You lied! You're like all of them, saying you want to help, but you were just trying to get away from me!"

Tiff's head spun as she tried to form words, but she was too terrified to speak.

Ted kicked her in the side with a booted foot and the air left her. She couldn't breathe as agony tore through her side.

He spun away from her, fisting his hands in his hair and screaming. Tiff couldn't follow any of it, her focus only on the fact she couldn't take in a breath. It was as if her lungs had locked up.

Then she remembered something Shauna had told her once when they were practicing self-defense moves during one of the classes they'd taken together. Shauna always knew as much or more than the instructors but she went with Tiff anyway, saying she wanted Tiff to be able to take care of herself.

"Breathe out, Tiff. Your body wants to suck in air but you need to breathe out!"

Tiff had caught an elbow to the chest by mistake and her lungs had locked up then, too.

Tiff closed her eyes now, listening to the words of her friend. She forced the air out of her lungs even though she didn't think there was any in there.

Her body responded and her lungs kicked back into gear, taking in the breath she so desperately needed.

Tiff watched Ted as he paced, muttering to himself under his breath.

When she thought she could speak, she did it carefully, as calmly as her shaking voice would allow.

"Ted, I was scared. You understand that, don't you? I didn't know what you wanted from me. I didn't think I could just sit and wait." She gambled on the next bit. "I didn't want to be a victim, Ted. You understand that, don't you?"

Would he realize he was victimizing her the same way

his sisters were victimized? Would he see what he was doing and stop?

He turned to her, his face a mask of anger, fists clenched.

He didn't come at her, though. He stayed where he was, chest heaving.

Tiff spoke again. "I have people I love, Ted. I want to get back to them safely." Ronan. She wanted to get back to him. She wanted to have a future with him. The man who didn't see her as too smart or too creepy because of her field of work. Who saw her as someone to respect and cherish. She wanted all of that.

"My grandmother is sick. She relies on me and I want to get back to her safely, but that doesn't mean I don't want to do what I promised. I meant it when I said your story should be told. Your story and Addie's and Ashley's. Even your baby brother's. He might not remember any of it the way you do, but he didn't deserve that start to his life. Something like that touches everyone involved. It's something no one should go through and hopefully, someday, no one will."

Tiff stopped speaking, waiting as Ted's breath heaved and his fists clenched and he seemed to wage a battle with the demons inside of him.

CHAPTER 30

THEY DIDN'T GO IN LIGHTS BLAZING. RONAN KNEW TED WAS A dangerous man who wouldn't hesitate to kill, and that meant he wouldn't hesitate to use Tiff as a shield if they startled him.

"I want a silent approach so we can get eyes on Ms. Carson and the suspect," he said into the radio, speaking to the detectives from Shauna's team who were tailing them.

The group was in agreement and they pulled off the road two minutes out from the location. As much as he wanted in there now, as much as he wanted Tiff back safe in his arms, they would do this right.

When they exited their vehicles, Shauna and her people approached, all of them suited up in body armor, ready to go.

Zach handed Ronan his vest and he donned it as Shauna spoke.

"I spoke with a connection at the FBI. They've got a negotiator an hour away on standby if we need her." She handed Ronan and Zach each an earpiece courtesy of her team so they could all communicate.

"We'll hike in from here," Ronan said, addressing all of them as he double- and triple-checked his ammo, weapon, and Taser. "Shauna, you and Hutch can take the back of the building. Zach and I will be out front."

He assigned the remaining detectives Shauna had brought to cover the sides of the building.

"I want recon. Let's see what we're dealing with and go from there. Nobody goes in unless I give the go-ahead, are we clear?"

He got nods all around.

They double-timed it to the site of the warehouses, taking in the four large metal buildings as they approached. Manny had been right. Two of them had suffered a lot of damage to the roofs and one had a large section of the upper part of one wall missing, like it had been shorn away by something.

One building was gutted from a fire, and though the metal still stood, it was blackened by the smoke, and the door they could see hung off the hinges. Metal building were meant to withstand fire, but apparently this one wasn't deemed worth cleaning up and repairing.

The building farthest from their position was largely intact, though its windows were boarded over and it didn't look like anyone had used it in years.

Ted Hadley's truck was parked crookedly on the concrete outside the door.

They'd found him. And that meant they had a shot at getting Tiff back.

Fuck that. It wasn't a shot. He would do it. Ronan was going to walk out of that building with Tiff.

He met the gazes of the other officers and tipped his head toward the final building.

He received nods all around and they moved in, walking

on near-silent feet to take up their positions.

When they neared the building, all but Zach peeled off to move around to the sides and back. He and Zach headed for the front door.

Zach covered Ronan as he studied the door. There were no crevices around it to let them see what was happening in there.

Ronan looked up. The windows were too high and peeling off those boards would make too much noise.

He scanned the area in front of them, checking all the places where there was wear on the metal. One area where the protective coating had worn away had begun to rust, and Ronan could see a small hole.

Moving to it, he bent and peered through it into the building.

As he did, he heard Shauna over his earpiece. She'd found a crack to look through on her side and was describing the same scene Ronan was looking at.

In the center of the large open space lay Tiff. She was bound to a toppled chair as Ted stood eight feet away.

Tiff was talking to him.

It looked like he was listening, but it was clear from the fact she was lying on her back that he'd gotten violent with her.

Ronan checked Ted's hands. No weapon.

Still, Ted was close enough to her that he could grab her before they could cross the space.

Ronan stood and let Zach look through so his partner would know what they were heading into.

Zach met Ronan's eyes, his expression grim. He knew what they were about to face. Knew how this could go.

Ronan spoke to the team through their comms, his eyes moving to the door. "We move on my count."

CHAPTER 31

Tiff watched Ted's face, praying he would see her as he saw his sisters. She weighed her words and knew she had to chance going directly at him with what he was doing.

"What your father did to your sisters was wrong. I know you're not like him. I know you wouldn't hurt an innocent person." She swallowed down the sick feeling of casting him as someone who hadn't harmed innocents, but she needed to make him think she believed his actions were justified.

"I know you don't want to make me a victim, Ted."

Her hands were shaking and her breaths were starting to come in short gasps as she tried to keep his gaze.

Ted opened his mouth, but the room around them exploded with noise and movement.

There was shouting as light spilled in from both sides, metal slamming against metal as doors were kicked in.

A swarm of people. Officers with guns drawn, shouting at Ted to get down. To lie down and put his hands over his head.

Ted dove for Tiff as shots rang out.

Tiff saw Ronan, strong and composed. She saw flashes from the barrels of weapons.

Ronan had fired, but he wasn't the only one. Ted landed on top of her, but he hadn't fallen there.

He had dived for her. And in her heart, Tiff knew, he'd been diving to cover her from the bullets. He'd been protecting her like he'd tried to do with his sisters so many years before.

As his body was dragged from hers, Ronan moved in, running his hands over her as the others moved Ted farther from her, kneeling to check for a pulse.

All of it happened around her. She took in bits and pieces of it, but mostly she cried.

For herself. For the fear and panic she'd felt. She cried in relief that Ronan was there. That she was safe.

But she also cried for Ted. She cried for his sisters. For the loss of their innocence and the horrific action they'd had to take when no one else would.

And Ronan held her.

EPILOGUE

IT WAS TRULY ASTOUNDING HOW MUCH LIFE COULD CHANGE IN a matter of months. Tiff was still haunted sometimes, thinking about how things could have gone in that warehouse if she hadn't been able to make Ted see her as he saw his sisters. If Ronan and the others hadn't made it to her in time.

Ted Hadley had died at the scene. Several of the detectives seemed skeptical of Tiff's theory that Ted had tried to protect her from the gunshots, but she was sure of it. He was a vicious killer, but he was also still that small kid trying to protect his sisters from harm.

His aunt was the only surviving member of the family, other than the two younger siblings who'd been placed into the system, but Nancy Renard had been arrested for her attempts to protect Ted.

Tiff couldn't help but think about the younger Howell children. It was possible the youngest wouldn't even know he was related to the Howells if he'd been adopted young in a closed adoption. If he saw reports of the violent end to his brother's life, would he even know who Ted was?

Ashley would, though. She was ten when she was adopted. She'd been raped by her father. She knew her brother and sister committed murder in her defense. If she saw what happened to Ted, she would know who he was. She would see what happened to the brother who stood up to the monster tormenting them all.

Tiff couldn't imagine what Ashley would feel to see what happened to her siblings.

But for now, Tiff tried not to think about it. Her dreams occasionally shifted into nightmares, recalling Ted hovering over her with his knife in hand, ready to slash her throat as he had done with his victims before her.

A part of her still heard his dying wish for her to tell his story. She might one day, but it was also her story now. Her tale of violence and survival, and separating the two enough to be able to write about his part of it might not be possible for her for a long time.

But, as is always the case, time went on. And with it came new reasons to be happy. To be grateful she'd survived and had a future to look forward to.

And Ronan Cafferty to hold onto when the nightmares came.

After years of focusing almost exclusively on her work, she was ready for more. Ronan had taken to sleeping on her couch at first, but after coming in often to soothe her after a bad dream, he now slept in her bed where he could hold her through the night.

She twisted in his arms now, turning to watch him as he held her. She expected to find his eyes closed, but they weren't. He was watching her, a heat in his eyes that rocked her.

They'd had some incredibly hot make-out sessions, but

they'd always stopped short of sex. Now, though, she didn't want to stop any longer. She wanted to share everything with this man. Body, mind, heart, and soul.

"Ronan," she whispered, drawing one leg up and over his hips as she pulled his face down to meet hers for a kiss.

He groaned and pulled her to him, and she forgot all about her nightmares as his kiss lit her up from head to toe. His large hands ran down her back and Tiff shifted, wanting more.

She moved till she was straddling him and looked down at her sexy detective. She couldn't help but smile.

"What's that smile about?" Ronan asked, his hands continuing to roam her body, making her squirm on top of him.

"I was remembering the way you shut me out when you found out I was a professor the first day we met. You wanted nothing to do with me."

She moved her hips on his, grinding her against him as her breath caught in her chest.

He groaned and pushed up into her. They still wore the clothes they planned to sleep in, and Tiff wanted them off. She wanted to feel him inside her.

She reached for the hem of her shirt to pull it off, but he trapped her hands against her stomach, holding them there. Damn this man and his control.

"The first day I met you, I wanted everything to do with you. You came into my office with this black hair," he said, running his hand down her hair and then brushing his hand over her cheek and nose. "These adorable freckles and that intensity and passion for what you do. I wanted all of it."

She laughed. "You did not. You were all gruff, jerky

detective man." She lowered her voice. "We can't possibly take any time out of our busy schedules. Don't you know we're important?"

He wrangled her hands so that one of his held her two smaller ones together. She should have been frightened to have someone pin her arms like that after what she'd been through but she wasn't. She trusted this man completely.

He took his other hand and began to stroke one of her nipples through the fabric, his touch so light it made her squirm again, pressing herself into his hand, seeking more.

"Are you making fun of me, Ms. Carson?" Ronan asked, his tone low and as teasing as his hand.

She gasped and pressed into him again. "I'll stop. I promise, just—"

"Just what, Tiff?" He pulled down the loose neck of her shirt to expose her nipple and closed his mouth around it. The heat ran through her, spreading to all the parts of her that so wanted this man's touch. His kiss.

She moaned.

"Hmm? What was that?"

"Damn you and your control, Ronan Cafferty."

Ronan's chuckle was throaty and deep, but he flipped her over and proceeded to give her just what she wanted. His hands and mouth. All of him, until she was climaxing beneath him and he was moving inside of her, calling out her name as he orgasmed himself.

Tiff slept in his arms afterward. If she had a nightmare that night, she didn't remember it. They didn't magically disappear, but it didn't matter. She could handle anything, especially with Ronan at her side.

.   .   .

Thank you so much for reading Wicked Justice! If you want more from the Sutton Capital world, go back to the beginning with The Billionaire Deal!

ABOUT THE AUTHOR

Lori Ryan is a NY Times and USA Today bestselling author who writes contemporary romance and romantic suspense. She lives with an extremely understanding husband, three wonderful children, and two dogs (who are lucky they're adorable and cute because they rarely behave) in Austin, Texas. It's a bit of a zoo, but she wouldn't change a thing.

Lori published her first novel in April of 2013 and has loved every bit of the crazy adventure this career has taken her on since then. Lori loves to connect with her readers. Follow her on Facebook or Twitter or subscribe to her blog. Oh, and if you've read Lori's books and loved them, please consider leaving a review with the retailer of your choice to help other readers find her work as well! It's a tremendous honor to have her work recommended to others or written up in reviews. Lori promises to do a happy dance around her office every time you write one!

You can sign up for Lori's newsletter here to keep in touch and get fun bonuses!